TANYA

TANYA

J.P. READING

SCHOLASTIC BOOK SERVICES
New York Toronto London Auckland Sydney

Copyright © 1976 by J. P. Reading. All rights reserved. Published by Scholastic Book Services, a division of Scholastic Magazines, Inc.

12 11 10 9 8 7 6 5 4 3 2   7 8 9/7 0 1/8

*For Gloucester
and Wally —
Who made everything possible*

CHAPTER
ONE

I felt chilled and frightened as I sat in the Port Authority Terminal on a September morning, waiting for my bus. It was a warmish day, I realized, and so obviously it was my nerves rather than the weather that were making me shake.

I snuggled deeper into my corduroy coat and reminded myself that nobody was forcing me to do this, and that I wasn't being punished. I tried to feel good about what I was about to do; I tried to remember how much I'd been hating New York and how happy I knew I was going to be living on the New England coast. I tried all these things — I even tried to smile. But I failed miserably. I've just never been very good

1

at convincing myself not to be frightened or to feel better about something I feel awful about. And this time was no exception. Why didn't they announce the bus? Why didn't someone sit down next to me and tell me her life's story, the way strangers in stations are supposed to do?

Since the commuter rush, it had grown very quiet; no public address announcements, no people bumping rudely into my knees and suitcases. There was just a weird mid-morning silence that made me believe for a moment that no buses were going to leave for anywhere ever, and that I was going to just sit here, getting all moldy and growing into the bench while people passed by and viewed me as an unclaimed oddity. Poor thing! Nowhere to go, just sought shelter here and grew hard as old cheese.

What a thought! I shook myself a bit, just to make sure I could still move, and decided to get up and hunt a cup of coffee. Maybe some warm liquid in my empty stomach would make me feel better.

The coffee, when I finally got it, was thick and black and disgusting, but at least holding the paper cup and drinking from it gave me something to do and warmed my icy fingers. After a few gulps and seeing some sign of life as a harried mother with a small child dashed past me, I began to feel a little better, and then I started to think about the unusual position I had put myself in.

Two weeks ago I was a disembodied voice over the phone, answering hundreds of questions a day for the information department of the New York Public Library. I had liked my job well enough in the beginning, but after two years the novelty of it had paled. I had begun to grow bored and irritable, looking up the batting averages of the New York Mets, finding out who first conducted Beethoven's Ninth Symphony, telling people O. Henry's real name, and in what city the first Continental Congress had been held.

Of course it did make good conversation at parties, but I am quite shy, and there were many parties and luncheons that no one ever got around to asking me to. So there I was. A fund of semi-useless information with a steady job that didn't promise much more than a barely adequate income.

Then one day as I was clearing up my desk and getting ready to go home, I decided to stop off at the reading room in the library and look up back copies of my hometown newspaper. I was feeling rather sentimental and lonely, and I thought it would warm me to read about some people I knew, and maybe even some I liked. Not too many of those would have liked me back, I reflected ruefully, gathering up my bag and coat, since I had been generally known as a smart aleck, too big for her you-know-whats, and just generally disagreeable. That's what comes of being shy, I grimaced to myself, and being afraid that nobody will like you. What you sometimes do then, in defense, is be such a stinker, that you are disliked for certain. My aunt, with whom I'd lived since my parents died, had called it "digging your own grave and lying in it." My aunt was not a very original person, I reflected, nor a very kind one.

I liked the reading room, all mellow light and dark wood. It made me feel cozy. But tonight the fans were whirring their way through a thick August heat wave, and the people scattered about at tables looked tired and sticky.

I wondered if I should have gone straight home, and then, since I was there, decided to look up the papers anyway. I flipped through a few, not finding anything or anyone interesting, and was just about to give it all up and leave, when I noticed a copy of a newspaper that someone hadn't bothered to put away.

"Inconsiderate," I muttered, reaching for the paper to return with my own, when I saw that it was a copy of the *Gloucester Daily Times*. I sat back down quickly and drew the paper toward me, feeling muzzy

4

and a little shaky. Gloucester, Massachusetts. My parents and I had spent two wonderful beautiful weeks up there when I was fourteen, the summer before they'd been killed in an automobile accident.

It had really been a perfect time, one of the happiest we'd ever known together. I opened the paper and began to read — loving all of it — the articles, features, editorials. How nice to be part of a community where people had time to care about birds and saving trees and building new animal shelters. It all swam before my eyes and gave me back a piece of that summer.

I read every word until I got to the car, house, and want ads. And then I read them too. And there it was. Stuck in between "waitress wanted" and "plumber's ass't. needed."

House-Sitter

Person needed, *desperately*, to care for our lovely West Gloucester home for one year. Duties simple. Beautiful location on Annisquam River. Semi-isolated. Ideal for writer, reader, gardener, almost anyone. Easy-living salary.

A phone number and hours to call followed. Without really thinking, just feeling terribly excited, I hastily got out a note pad and jotted the number down. Then I tidied up the library table and went home.

I didn't even look at the number again until the next morning. I was afraid that I was going to do something crazy and impulsive, and then when I got up on Saturday to a sizzling hot city day, with trucks rumbling and honking outside, I was sure of it.

I got out of bed and walked to the window. Below me the city, or at least a narrow, dirty street of it, baked in the sun. A skinny cat prowled the gutter, an old man spit on a stoop, and two grubby children were banging sticks on the wrought-iron fence of the convent across the street. Wouldn't it be lovely to leave here, I mused. And then I thought, of course, why not try to do it.

Bypassing a few warnings that shot up in my mind, like what are you going to do when the year is up, I moved across the room, picked up the telephone, and began to dial.

Suddenly a voice was saying hello and my ears were buzzing as I answered.

"Hello, my name is Tanya Sohier, and I'm calling to answer your ad for a house-sitter."

"Oh, how nice," breathed a friendly voice at the other end, and I began to feel comfortable. "My husband and I were just beginning to despair. We expected to get a lot of calls, but the only response we've gotten so far was from a young boy who thought it was funny to tell me that he'd certainly house-sit for us. Every day after school he'd climb up on our roof and sit on the chimney till dinnertime!"

I laughed and so did she. "That's pretty good," I said, "but probably not what you had in mind."

"Not quite."

"Well," and now I was uncertain again, "I'm not sure what you'll want to know about me." I paused. "I don't live in Gloucester, I'm calling from New York, but I saw the ad in the *Gloucester Daily Times*, and I thought that maybe getting out of New York for a year was just the thing I wanted to do."

There was silence for a moment, and then, "New York? Oh, well that would be difficult, I think. I mean we'd need to meet you first and settle some things. . . ." The voice trailed off, and I stood by the phone, dumb, all confidence gone, not being able to think of a thing to say. Why hadn't I realized how ridiculous all of this was anyway?

"Oh, wait a minute! I've just remembered! My husband is going to be in New York next week. That is, I'm almost sure he is. Raymond! Hold on a minute, will you." And distantly I could hear footsteps and talking. Oh, maybe, I found myself thinking, maybe it really will work out. And I felt a rush of pleasure shoot up my back.

"Hello, Miss Sohier? You still there?"

"I'm here."

"Good. Well, listen, I was right. Raymond, my husband, is going to be in the City next Tuesday. Can I give him your number and have him call and arrange a meeting with you?"

"Yes, of course," I told her happily, and relayed my work number and home number, just stopping short of adding my social security number, measurements, and birthdate.

And "Oh," she laughed right before hanging up, "I'm sorry. I haven't even told you our names! Rinn. Raymond and Anne. Does that do everything all right?"

It did everything perfectly for me, and I moved through three days of steamy New York humidity all glazed-over happy. Of course they were certain to want me, weren't they?

On Tuesday morning, I was a little less confident and a lot more nervous. I got up early so I could take a bath and dress. In case Mr. Raymond Rinn called and wanted to see me right away, I would be ready.

In the tub, door open in case the phone

8

should ring — at six thirty! — I relived, as I'd been doing for the last few days, all I remembered about Gloucester and New England. Thick, leafy trees and pines with church steeples rising out of them, natural stone fences warming in the sun, great boulders hugging sand as the sea crashed against them, old Victorian houses with gables and turrets, people who smiled on the street and stopped to talk. What a fine change all that would be from the smell of garbage in my hallway and the constant daily battle I had with legions of cockroaches in my dingy little room. Also I would be leaving the library, and I was certainly ready to do that.

I got out of the tub with my heart pumping, straining to hear the phone, willing it to ring. Despite the weather I dressed in a long-sleeved white silk blouse and a red pants suit which clashed superbly with my orange hair. Not too bad, I thought, looking in the mirror and arranging my neck-length hair to look windblown. Now just a pair of sunglasses and I'll certainly look old enough to handle a house. I was nervous, but I also felt kind of cocky, which was unusual for me — for the rather reticent person who always lurked somewhere inside.

The phone call didn't come till eleven o'clock, and by that time I'd gotten myself into a terrible state and was beginning to wonder for the first time what it was that I was getting into. A state, a town, a house I knew nothing about. Scratch the steeples and the sunny blue waves from your mind, Tanya, I warned, feeling my heart jerk against my blouse as the phone pealed out at me.

Why should this be him? My phone rang constantly; why this particular moment? But I knew it was and I answered in an uneven, high-pitched voice.

Mr. Rinn sounded kind and gentle, if you can get that from just a "hello, how are you?" and I relaxed a little.

We arranged to meet at an Italian restaurant, not far from where I worked. I barely had time to fix what little makeup I wear, to rewindsweep my hair, and get to the restaurant a slim two minutes before him.

"No wonder you told me I'd recognize you by your hair," smiled a tall nice-looking man coming up to me on the crowded New York street and holding out his hand.

We escaped into the dim coolness New York provides for summer-weary workers, and managed to get what seemed to be the last table, in a corner right near the swinging kitchen doors. All during lunch, which somehow was pleasant and unscary, we were assailed by the odors of garlic and various sauces wafting out to us.

"The one thing I don't understand," Mr. Rinn, or "Raymond," said, "is why a young girl like you should want to come up and live all alone in a house in a relatively small town, for a year."

"That's easy," I said, swallowing a gluey mouthful of spaghetti and wondering what he'd tell his wife about the restaurant I'd picked. "I really don't like New York at all. I want to look out a window and see trees and flowers, maybe even birds and a glimpse of water." I smiled at him. "I think that it'll be easier for me to get involved in things too, living in a small town I mean. New York offers so much, so constantly, that I never really get to doing anything at all." And as I said those words, I saw how really true they were.

Raymond glanced around the crowded room, at the jostling waiters with irritated masks for faces, and the customers, equally annoyed, demanding service, and then looked back at me.

"I don't have any trouble understanding that, I guess."

And so we spoke about practical things like salary and dates, and in a short time we were both outside, shaking hands and telling each other we'd meet again in three weeks.

As I headed back to the library I floated

free. This was it then, this was the beginning. Oh, Tanya, my dear, you are a lucky young woman, I thought, and stopped to treat my gray metal desk to a huge bunch of zinnias.

When I got back to the office I arranged the flowers in an old jam jar someone had left lying about, and murmured aloud, although no one heard me, "In just three weeks someone else will be sitting at this desk," and I realized I was grinning all over my face — just like Alice's cat.

CHAPTER
TWO

Remembering my first flush of exhilaration, I wondered why I was having to spoil it now by being so jittery and feeling all kinds of trepidations like: You're going to be lonely, miserable, and unhappy. What do you know about living in a small town and taking care of a house? What if there's a fire? And a lot more what-ifs that I hadn't allowed myself to feel during the last few weeks. My hands started to perspire through their chunky coldness.

"All passengers for New Haven, Hartford, and Boston may now board at Gate 92. Express bus leaving for Boston at ten thirty."

I got up with relief, picking up my two heavy suitcases and heading for Gate 92.

Well here it is, whatever it is, I thought wryly as I boarded the bus, a book clamped under my arm and my hair escaping from a scarf and streaking into my eyes.

The book, along with an uncomfortable and unexpected lunch, had been a gift from the info staff at the library. It was a collection of Jane Austen's novels and I'd thought it very unimaginative of them. But last night, when I'd been having a rotten time trying to fall asleep, I decided to sit up and read, and discovered that rereading Jane Austen was soothing and lovely, particularly because it allowed me to escape from myself.

The lunch had been another thing entirely, purely an afterthought, and an embarrassing one too.

I'd spent my last morning in the library signing forms and clearing up things for my replacement. Around noon, just as I was on my way out for a hot dog, Elizabeth and Jennie, two coworkers, stopped at my desk with the tissue-wrapped book, accompanied by one of those from-the-whole-bunch cards with the usual cluster of grapes on the front of it.

They seemed uncomfortable as Jennie put the package down in front of me.

"Listen, Tanya . . ."

"I know. Good-bye and good luck, right?" I said, not knowing what to say, hearing myself sound brusque, and coloring a little because of it.

They pasted smiles on their faces for me as I unwrapped their gift and gave what I hoped was a delighted exclamation.

"This is really nice," I said, trying. "My mind could use some sterner stuff than it's been accustomed to." But when I saw their expressions, I was immediately sorry. I'd been making a lot of caustic remarks lately about the fund of superficial information acquired working for a reference service.

"No, really, this is great," I tried amending.

"We hoped you'd find it a relief from the trivia we have to deal with here," said Elizabeth, who is a very stiff person.

"Well, I will. I'm sure I will," I answered, feeling very foolish about this conversation and hoping I could think of some way to end it.

But they both just stood there, not knowing how to leave, asking questions about what exactly I was going to be doing, most of which had already been asked and answered.

"Ralph and Caroline should be here too," Jennie remarked, looking over her shoulder at the obviously empty room. She paused, and then seemed unable to add anything. I waited too, wondering why it was that I so often inspired silence and awkwardness.

"Well," I said at last, shoving out from my desk, "I'm starved." This was not in the least true, but it was the only exit I could think of.

They looked at each other. It was the kind of look two people give thinking that the third person is either oblivious or blind. Oh no, oh no, I thought, panicky, they think it's a hint, or an invitation or something. They think I want them to take me out. And they did.

We went to a Chinese restaurant and ate spare ribs and egg rolls, I, at least, with a chalky throat. Jennie insisted we have a glass of plum wine. All we would have needed to look totally miserable were some paper hats and noisemakers.

I sank into a cushiony seat by a window and delighted in the steamy heat warming the side of the bus. It must have been at least eighty out, but I was still freezing.

As the driver gunned the engine and we moved into midtown traffic, I reminded myself that there was no turning back now. At least not until New Haven.

Once on the expressway, the combination of heat, scarf, and coat began to make me sleepy, and I half dozed for about an hour. It was the kind of sleep when you're really not, and a kaleidoscope making crazy images kept forming, dissolving, and reforming in my head. It was a very anxious way of dreaming, a jangling experience, making me more tired than ever.

I awoke exhausted, and determined that I would read more Jane Austen, to see if she could be the same balm to me now that she'd been last night.

I settled down and tried to relax, and it almost worked. By the time the bus reached Hartford, I decided I was just going through a kind of stage fright, which would blow away as soon as I smelled salt air.

After Hartford I was too excited to concentrate on *Emma*, so I closed my book and looked out the window. Soon we were swinging onto the Massachusetts Turnpike, and then the scenery held all my attention. The countryside had become rougher when we crossed the state line. Granite rocks lined the road; cattails grew beside bogs; and flame-colored tree flew past me. I was almost sorry when buildings began to replace the trees and I realized that we must be approaching Boston.

Raymond had told me that either he or his wife would pick me up at the bus station and drive me to their home on Cape Ann. I took out my makeup case and tried to dare my face into looking sensible. I'm not pretty, and looking at myself now I wondered when I would really come to terms with that. I brushed my hair (which really was pretty, and shouldn't have belonged to me at all) into sharp bangs and pushed it with my fingers so that it curved around my ears. Then I applied a light shade of lipstick to my too wide mouth, and after quickly smacking my cheeks with a powder puff I was finished. So you're not quite Glenda Jackson. I made a face at myself. So what?

When I got off the bus my throat felt dry and I was swallowing a lot, but at least I wasn't obviously trembly. The bus station was quite small, so I didn't think I'd have any trouble meeting them. However, in ten minutes I was pretty certain that there wasn't a Rinn around to pick me up. Every woman I looked hopefully at, thinking maybe this was Anne, looked busily in another direction. And there was no sign of Raymond.

Then, just as I was beginning to get quaky again, I felt a hand on my arm and found myself looking directly into a pair of light blue eyes, asking a question of me from a rounded, smiling face.

"You're Tanya Sohier. You must be," she said. "Raymond told me about your hair." She laughed. "Oh, of course other things too. Listen, I'm really sorry I'm late. I'd like to give you a good excuse, but the truth is I forgot what time you were coming, and then when I remembered I was already late."

She had taken one of my suitcases and was propelling me out of the waiting room with no great speed. "Does that ever happen to you? I mean you get all involved in something, and you hardly know where you are?" Anne did not wait for an answer. "That's what I did with my morning. I started to read *Future Shock* — I'm just getting around to that now; everyone else has already read it! And I didn't even do the dishes, or make the beds, and I almost didn't come for you."

"I know what you mean," I managed, glad to say something and show her I had a voice.

Anne stopped still for a moment and looked directly at me. "Oh, listen, I'm sorry! I haven't let you say a word, have I? Raymond says it's my main fault. I always do all the talking. I never just shut up and listen. Okay, well now I'm going to shut up and give you a chance."

I liked Anne Rinn, I knew that immediately, but right now she was making me nervous. What was I supposed to talk about? I wished she would just go on saying whatever she was saying, so that I could listen, and not feel that anything was expected of me.

I tried smiling at her. "I'm really glad to be here," was the super comment I came up with.

"And we're so glad and relieved to have

you." She took my arm as if we'd known each other for a long time. "My car's just over there. The banged up one. You'll prefer driving Raymond's — it's all sleek and blue. You *can* drive, can't you? And Raymond did tell you that the car or the cars, whichever one you'd prefer, were for you to use?"

"Yes, he did." She must think I'm a real dummy, I thought. If I were Anne Rinn I wouldn't leave my house with a monosyllabic idiot.

But she didn't seem to be noticing, and her conversation had a good effect on me. I leaned back in the car seat, fairly relaxed for me, and prepared to enjoy the ride.

"We're only about an hour out of Boston, barring traffic," Anne chatted, "and it's a pretty ride, once you get on to Route 128."

The hour went quickly. I found my tongue and was able to add little parenthetical remarks to Anne's conversation, and so by the time she said, "This is our turn-off, right here," I was remarkably at ease, and happily expectant.

"Oh, it's beautiful," I told her, looking out of my window at old houses tucked up in brownish-green lawns. There were picket fences, pumpkins set on porches, and an occasional bunch of Indian corn tacked on a front door.

"Does it seem familiar at all?" Anne asked, handling the curves and dips in the road with skill.

Her question stopped me. I had forgotten for a little while that I had been here before, six years ago. The sudden memory, forced back, made my eyes prick. "No," I told her, careful of my voice. "I'm not remembering any of this, I don't think."

Anne glanced at me quickly. "Raymond told me about your parents. I'm so sorry, Tanya, it must have been terrible for you."

"Yes," I said shakily, amazed that after six years I could still feel as if someone were jumping on my stomach with a pair of cleated boots.

"Here we are, right up this lane," and as Anne swung to the left I caught a glimpse of a three-storied white wood house that seemed to be filled with windows. It was partly obscured by two giant oaks, glowing against the light clapboard.

"It's lovely, Anne," I told her as we drove up to a grassy space beside the house. "But I had no idea it would be so big," I burst out.

"Oh, don't let that worry you. The rooms are actually quite small, in fact a few of them we just use for storage. And you can be the same sloppy housekeeper I am. *Please*," she told me sternly, "don't worry about cleaning. Just a soft occasional dust rag will do it. Raymond says I have a rotten pair of eyes, but the house never looks dirty to me."

"After living in a furnished room for almost two years, anything to do with your house will most probably be a pleasure," I said, aware of sounding slightly formal. I hoped she hadn't thought I was about to complain. After the nice salary they were paying me, it would be no hardship to clean, thoroughly clean, I told myself, at least once a week.

The two days before Anne and Raymond were to leave for their year in Europe went by in a rush of instructions. Anne was constantly remembering something she had forgotten to remind me about, and Raymond had a lot of practical advice about oil-burners, fuses, and things similarly unknown to me.

"I think," Raymond said the afternoon before they left, "that we'd better just sit down today and write Tanya a list. By now we must have her thoroughly confused."

"Oh, no, I'll be all right," I tried to reassure him, as Anne groaned, "Ah, no, not a list, Raymond. I hate lists; I always forget to put anything important on them."

"Then I'll do the list," he said. And when he handed it to me that evening I was staggered.

Anne looked over my shoulder. "Raymond, this is ridiculous. Look at Tanya, she's all white and shaking just *looking* at this thing."

"I'm not," I said, embarrassed. "It looks ... fine."

They both stared at me.

"Well, a little forboding," I laughed. "I think I'm going back to New York."

It was wonderful for me to feel so free with the two of them. That night as I got into bed I found myself wishing that they weren't going away at all. That the three of us could just live together in this house for the next year or twelve. It was so rare for me to have an easy rapport with people. And now, just as I had achieved it, they were going away. Inadvertently my thoughts swung to my parents, and hot tears slid down my cheeks. "Oh, cut it out will you?" I whispered aloud, turning over and gazing at the tracery of dark leaves against my window. But I knew what had happened. Since my parents had died, there hadn't been anyone I'd been as comfortable with as I was with Anne and Raymond. And now I was going to lose them too. This thinking is foolishness, I rebuked myself. When the Rinns get back from Europe you can find a job right here in Gloucester if you want to, and the three of you can live happily ever after. Soothing myself with those thoughts, I finally fell asleep.

I awoke the next morning to a gray, weepy-looking day. Wind was wooshing around the house and rain splashed against my bedroom windows.

The room was chilly, despite the fact that I hadn't opened any windows, and I pulled my knees up to my chest and burrowed more deeply into the bedclothes. I was conscious of not wanting to get up to face the day and have to say good-bye.

I looked at my watch. Seven o'clock and the house was quiet. I'd hurry and fix breakfast to surprise them, I decided, bravely throwing off my quilt and shivering into my clothes. Maybe I'd better start by looking at the heat, I thought, tiptoeing downstairs.

By the time Anne and Raymond were up, an hour later, I had the table set for breakfast and had managed to conquer the waffle-maker.

They were both pleased, and made all sorts of nice noises at me, but I could see that their minds were already on the trip. Anne could hardly sit still for excitement, and Raymond was smiling at everything for no particular reason.

"Oh, I know something we haven't told you," Anne said, biting down on a crunchy piece of bacon: "about the people next door." She swallowed thoughtfully. "And I guess the reason I didn't is that we don't know anything about them really."

"Well, that clears that up," Raymond remarked drily.

"Next door?" I asked her. "You mean that dark brown house you can see from the side lawn?" I was used to next door either being attached or an arm's length away.

"Yes," Anne told me, "they really are our closest neighbors, but we hardly know them. The Freddies, a lovely old couple, lived there up until about a month ago. And when they moved, these people, the Harrises, moved in. I went over one afternoon to see them, but they weren't very friendly."

"You mean you burst in and babbled at them for an hour or so and then wondered why they didn't immediately invite you to stay for dinner," Raymond remarked.

"I did not," Anne shot at him. "I mean that they were just strange. I told you that, Raymond."

"But you think that everybody who isn't warm and inviting is strange."

"Well, maybe." Anne played with her fork. "Anyhow, she seemed kind of hyper, and he's one of those big bruising men, who like you to know how really rough they are. And I think they have a little girl, only I didn't see her."

"But I bet you tried." Raymond grinned at his wife.

"Well, I did," she confessed, "but all I saw were some dolls and toys lying around. Anyhow, Tanya, don't let me influence you — "

"Heaven forbid!" her husband interrupted, and Anne made a face at him.

"I mean that," she said. "I'm always jumping to conclusions about people, and they're usually the wrong ones. But if you do get to meet them," Anne brightened, "be sure and write me all about it, okay?"

"Okay," I told her, hoping that I would find she was wrong.

I saw little more of Anne and Raymond until they were ready to leave. Some friends were to drive them to the airport, and I was very conscious of not having been invited to go along. It's probably because they thought it would be a bore for me, I tried to reassure myself, and then wondered if maybe I should have *asked* to go. But it was too late to do that now.

"You *will* write, Tanya, won't you?" Anne asked, just before they left. "And you are pleased about staying here? I mean it won't seem too lonely to you or anything?"

"This is a fine time to ask her that," Raymond observed.

But Anne paid no attention. "There'll be all kinds of groups starting up in the fall, remember. Poetry, sketching, rap sessions.

You'll really find plenty to do, just check the *Times* every day, and then of course Boston is so close, but you've had enough of that big-city living, haven't you."

"I have indeed," I told her, trying to arrange my face so that I would not give in to tears. How stupid they would think I was, crying at their leaving after I'd only known them two days!

"Anne," Raymond reminded her, "the Kerrs have been waiting in the car for almost fifteen minutes."

"Oh, I know, I know," she said, looking around her and then back to me, "it's just that now that it's really time to leave I don't want to go. I think I'd rather just stay here with Tanya and the house. Dear old house. I do love it!"

"You always say that," Raymond told her, coming over to take my hand in both of his, "even when we're just going away for a weekend."

"Oh, I know," Anne wailed, and suddenly threw her arms around me and hugged me hard, so that we were all a jumble of hands and bodies. And then we were laughing and Anne got a little teary just as Raymond managed to whisk her out the door and plant a swift, shy kiss on my cheek. "Take care," he said, and I nodded hard at him.

I stepped outside and waved to them

furiously until the car was well out of sight. I felt like a marionette whose arm was being jerked, but I just dreaded the thought of going inside to a house that I knew was going to feel terribly empty.

I'll do something right away, I thought. I'll check the kitchen and then I'll go into town and shop, and then I'll have lunch and then I'll read a book, and then . . . the hours and days stretched emptily ahead of me.

I finally closed the door against the misty, desolate-looking day and walked through the hall and into the kitchen, my footsteps echoing in the too-silent house.

CHAPTER
THREE

Shopping was fun, or maybe it was just the idea that I was running a house now and could be as creative as I liked. It only took me about half an hour to get acquainted with all the stores in Gloucester, and I decided I would do most of my grocery shopping at Collinses, as Anne had suggested. It had a warm, townish feeling which was nicer than the big glittering supermarket.

It was sort of strange introducing myself to Mr. and Mrs. Collins and telling them I'd be staying at the Rinns' home while they were away. But Anne had suggested that too, and the Collinses were both so friendly and chatty that it wasn't as difficult as I had expected.

When I came out of their store I stood gazing at a view of the harbor, and memories stirred in me. Ahead were washes of gray—the sea rolling into the horizon and blending with the overcast sky. Fishing boats bobbled in the water and gentle white-caps lapped against pilings. Imagine, I mused, coming out of Macy's and being confronted with something like this.

I wondered if the people who lived on Cape Ann really saw it at all, or if it had become to them what taxi cabs, screaming fire engines, and littered streets were to me.

I would have liked to walk along the wharves at leisure, just smelling the heavy fishy air and listening to the screams of the gulls, but my arms were heavy with packages and a steady rain had begun to fall again. I reluctantly headed for the car, promising myself that I would be back either as soon as the rain stopped or as soon as I had gotten myself a slicker.

As I drove the winding leaf-plastered road back to the Rinns, I felt very much in tune with everything about me. It had been wise of me to get out and do something, I reflected. If I had just sat around in the house I would have been mooning and sniffling by now.

When I got back, I took my time putting all my purchases neatly away, gazing happily at the knotty pine kitchen cupboards and the red tiled floor. What a treat this house was going to be, I thought, my spirits lifting considerably.

As I fried myself an egg for lunch, the skies began to clear and a spot of sunlight came into the kitchen and settled on Anne's African violet on the windowsill.

I gulped my egg down quickly, wanting to get outdoors and see about the marigold flats that Raymond had left in the shed for me to plant.

The sun was warm and sparkling on the river behind the house and I forgot all about the marigolds, just standing there and taking it all in — the fresh smell of wet earth, trees moving in a slight sea breeze. I sighed with contentment.

"Hello, Miss, would you like a kitten?" a voice spoke quite near and made me jump.

"What?" I exclaimed, looking down at a little girl, who was maybe ten years old, with streaky blonde hair and a thin, lonely looking face.

"Did I frighten you?" she asked.

"Well, yes, you did."

"I'm sorry. I thought you heard me coming." She hung her head slightly and I was conscious of not being very friendly.

"My name is Tanya," I told her. "Who are you?"

"Kate Harris. I live over there," she

sketched with her hand over to the side lawn of the house. "Is this where you live?" she asked me.

"No. I don't live here, I'm only staying here while the Rinns are away."

"Oh," was all she said, and I thought our conversation had come to a standstill. She's shyer than I am, I thought, and then realized how happy Anne would be to learn that there was indeed a daughter and I had gotten to know her.

"What was that about a kitten?" I asked, more for something to say than for anything else. Kate was a child, but it would be nice to talk to someone for a while anyhow, and since I didn't exactly have a group to pick from . . .

She brightened at the mention of the cat. "Oh, Miss . . . I'm sorry, I don't know your last name." She was very formal for such a small child.

"It's Sohier," I told her, "but you call me Tanya, okay?"

She smiled, which made her face look so radiant that it took me back a little. "All right," and then she launched into talking about her kitten.

"My father won't let me keep him. He doesn't like cats, and he said he won't even have a baby one around the house. I have to get rid of him, and I don't want to just let him go loose. He's too young; he'd just die," she finished, and I saw that her lips were trembling.

I cast about for some way to reassure her. "Well, don't you have any friends that might like to have a kitten?" I asked hopefully, afraid I might be getting trapped when I didn't know a thing about animals.

"I don't have any friends. We just moved here, and I don't know anyone."

"That's too bad," I said, "but I'm sure you'll meet other little girls soon, at school," I added.

"Well, there is my new little brother," Kate considered, "but he's too young to play with. He can't even talk yet. And besides, I couldn't give *him* my kitten, could I?" she laughed, and I was pleased to hear a happy sound come from her.

"Not very well, being that you're in the same house," I responded with a grin.

"So will you?" she asked me.

"Will I what?" I answered blankly.

"The kitten," Kate reminded me patiently. "Will you take the kitten?"

"Kate, I don't think I really could. . . ." I began, not quite knowing how to refuse and feeling a little mean.

"Why not?" she wanted to know. "You have this whole big house and all, and he's only a little kitten. His name is Peabody," she went on, "because I found him when my mother and I were shopping in Peabody. You'll love him. Wait just a minute and I'll get him for you."

"Kate, no, wait," I called out to her, but she was already running across the lawn, and if she heard me at all, she didn't look back.

Now what do I do? I asked myself, wandering around to the side of the house where I could watch Kate coming back from the Harrises. What could I tell her when she came back with the cat?

And then I thought that maybe it wouldn't be so bad after all. Having a kitten. It would be another living thing in the house anyway. At least I could try it, I decided, knowing I was being cowardly because I wasn't sure how to say no to Kate.

I looked over in the direction of the Harrises, expecting and dreading to see Kate come out at any moment. What I did see was a young, fair-headed child sitting on a blanket at the side of their house. A woman, whom I supposed was Mrs. Harris, was sitting beside him, and something about the picture they made struck me as being odd. At first I couldn't think what it might be, and then I realized it was the complete stillness of the two. They were both just sitting there, doing nothing. The child had no toys about him, and he sat with his legs thrust in front of him like a statue. Mrs. Harris was equally as quiet, only turning her head every once in a while to look down at her son. No picture of happy young motherhood there, I thought, and looked away, not liking the scene and wondering what about it bothered me.

Just then I heard a door slam and looked up to see Kate come pelting toward me, a ball of fluffy orange and white fur nestled in her arm.

"Here he is," she said breathlessly, "here's Peabody. You will call him that too, won't you . . . Tanya?" She seemed shy about using my name, or maybe it was just the prospect of actually giving her kitten away.

"I certainly will," I told her, reaching gingerly for the kitten. "But you're going to have to help me with him. Why don't you come in with me now and tell me what to feed him and how to take care of him." I held the soft little face up to me and was pleased to discover that I was enchanted as Peabody opened his mouth for a huge yawn.

"I don't think I should come in with you," Kate said, glancing uneasily over her shoulder, "my parents don't like me to . . . annoy anyone."

"That's nonsense, you wouldn't be annoying me. I need your help." I glanced back over at the Harris' lawn and was amazed to see that mother, child, and blanket had vanished. "Was that your little brother out there?"

Kate just looked at me.

"Just now," I explained, wondering how she could have failed to notice them, "with your mother. They were sitting on the lawn."

"Well, I guess I could come in for a little while," Kate said, and I wondered if she were ignoring me, or if she just hadn't heard. Anyhow I wasn't going to ask her again. It seemed foolish since the answer was so obvious.

Kate and I spent a pleasant half hour together discussing Peabody as he roamed the house, exploring. I had a momentary twinge when I wondered if Anne and Raymond would mind an animal in their house. But I decided they wouldn't, and anyhow, I would write them about it.

When Kate left, I made a flying trip back into Gloucester for some cat food and Kitty Litter. I wasn't so sure about the Litter but Kate had seemed very apprehensive when I suggested it would be all right to let Peabody out from time to time, so I decided I'd better get some.

"Back so soon, Miss Sohier," Mrs. Collins greeted me, "you forget something?"

"Not really," I smiled, "but I just acquired a kitten from the Harris' little girl, and I'll need some food."

"That's right, they're your neighbors, aren't they?" she said, reaching up to a shelf in back of her. "You know them?"

"Well, no, not really," I replied, "I just met Kate, their daughter, today. She had a kitten her father didn't want her to keep, and so — " I shrugged helplessly, every bit the innocent patsy. Now why had I done that? I was already fond of Peabody. Why was I making myself look put-upon to Mrs. Collins? Probably just because you didn't know what else to say, dope, I told myself, and decided I ought to think things out a little more before just reacting.

But Mrs. Collins was going on with her own thoughts. "Funny people, those," she told me. "Never come into town to shop. Must go somewhere else, but I can't think why they'd bother."

It was just a statement — colorless and uninquiring, but it made me wonder a bit more about the Harrises. I tried dismissing them from my mind; there was no need for me to be friendly with anyone but Kate if I didn't want to.

The sun was sinking down on the river in a fierce orange glow as I arrived home. What a nice day this has been after all, I reflected as I entered the house and Peabody jumped toward me and pressed his warm body against my legs.

"Are you hungry, sweetie?" I asked stooping to pet him. "Well, if you're not hungry, I bet you're cold," I said, standing. "Should we have a fire tonight, or do you think it's too early in the year?"

But I thought a fire would be nice. "That is," I told Peabody, "if I can decipher Raymond's instructions on how to start one."

And then I laughed at myself. "Crazy old Tanya Sohier, living in the woods and talking to her cat."

Nevertheless I felt cozy and pleased with myself as I put away Peabody's supplies and prepared to lay a fire for us in the living room fireplace.

I made myself a light meal, opened a can of foul-smelling tuna for Peabody, and decided that we would both eat in the living room with low lights and the warm flames of the fire that I was very proud of having gotten to kindle with the help of a Cape Cod lighter.

As I watched Peabody daintily but hungrily eat his fish glop, I remembered what Mrs. Collins had said about the Harrises not shopping in town. Funny that she would have known, I thought, and guessed I was too used to living in New York where you could shop at the same deli for years and the man behind the counter would still give you the identical blank stare each time, as if he'd never laid eyes on you before. This was much nicer, I decided, and then my thoughts again turned to the Harrises and I wondered idly why they didn't shop in Gloucester.

I watched Peabody sitting by his empty

bowl, giving himself a good washing, when something Anne had said nudged at me. Something about whenever I felt like seeing a movie, Peabody had some awfully good theaters. Peabody. I looked down at him again and remembered Kate saying that she'd given him that name because she'd found him when she and her mother were shopping in Peabody.

I jumped up and went over to the wall where the Rinns had a framed parchment map of Massachusetts, and traced around the north-shore area until I found Peabody. From the scale, I saw that it must be at least fifteen miles away. Mrs. Harris went all the way to Peabody to shop? Well, maybe she did. So what? Maybe there were more interesting stores in Peabody. Why was I spending any time even thinking about it? Probably because the Harrises seemed rather unusual to me. That, coupled with what Anne had said . . .

Yet that was most likely not the reason at all. Loneliness and the sudden and complete absence of people was making my mind focus on the Harrises. I shivered. If I were lonely tonight, how was I going to be for three hundred and sixty-four more nights?

"It's time for bed," I said aloud, and the kitten looked up at me in surprise.

"Well, it is," I told him, "because all of a sudden I'm feeling tired and I think I'm going to start crying." I scooped Peabody up and held him to me. It was nice to feel his sandpapery tongue graze against my cheek.

I cleaned the kitchen up quickly, trying not to think that it was only nine o'clock, and yawning to convince myself that I really *was* sleepy.

I climbed into bed with one of Raymond's mysteries. Tonight I needed something lighter and less demanding than Jane Austen.

After a half hour or so I began to feel sleepy. Peabody was curled up around my knees and I decided to let him stay there. His warmth was a comfort. I flicked off the light, and just as I was sliding gently out of consciousness something else Kate had said surfaced in my mind. It was about the little robotlike child I had seen sitting out on the lawn with Mrs. Harris. What was it? I fought sleep off trying to remember, and finally I did. She'd called him my "new" brother. New? What an odd . . . that baby, toddler, or whatever, had to be at least two. And if he were that old he couldn't possibly be new to Kate. Maybe she meant young, or little, my drowsy mind supplied a possible answer. And then I gave up fighting to stay awake.

I awoke to darkness and felt as if I had not slept at all. But when I looked at the little clock on my bedside table it said three A.M. I missed Peabody's coziness against my legs and wondered where he'd gone to. Just as I was patting around on the bed for him, I heard the sounds that must have awakened me.

At first I thought it was somebody calling out in the night. Definitely raised voices. I got up quickly and then I saw Peabody, crouched on my windowsill looking out into the darkness. I joined him there, raising the window slightly so I could hear better.

My bedroom was on the side of the house facing the Harrises, and I realized that that was where the sounds were coming from. I thought it was a man's voice I heard, shouting, but I couldn't make out the words. And somehow I didn't want to. I found that I was shaking and my feet, on the bare floorboards, were freezing. "Come away," I told Peabody, pulling down the window and drawing the curtains, "this has nothing to do with us."

But now I was shaking as if I had a fever. I reached for my robe and decided to go downstairs, turning on lights as I went. I wanted to get to the other side of the house, where that voice, with its harsh, ugly sound, wouldn't reach me.

I went into Raymond's den, turned the television on, and sat down stiffly on the couch. In moments Cary Grant's face swam before me on the screen. I couldn't pay much attention to what he was saying, but at least his was the only voice I was able to hear. In a little while my shaking had almost stopped and I rebuked myself for having gotten so frightened, settling back more comfortably on the couch and drawing an afghan around me. Peabody hopped up and stretched out comfortably on my legs.

After watching the movie for a while, I allowed myself to wonder why I'd gotten so scared. After all, I'd heard a lot worse shouting than that in New York. I'd often been awakened from sleep by hysterical people arguing and fighting in apartments on my street. It had become a not unusual occurrence to me. And, after the fascination and horror of the first time, I'd always just turned over and gone back to sleep, with a pillow over my head to blot out the noise.

I really had overreacted, I decided. People scream at each other in Gloucester as well as in New York, I told myself. It was just that I hadn't expected to find anything like that here, that was all.

But still, cowardice or whatever, I knew that I would spend my first night alone right here on the couch, with the comforting murmurs of Cary Grant lulling me to sleep.

CHAPTER FOUR

The next few days were peaceful enough. With a few false starts, I got used to living on my own, and was even beginning to enjoy it. I set in Raymond's marigolds, biked around Cape Ann, and went walking in Dogtown Common, which was a near wilderness where once witches had been reputed to have lived.

I hoped to see Kate again, at least to give her a glowing report on Peabody, but even though I dawdled around outside when I thought she might be coming home from school, I never got a glimpse of her. I even considered going over to the Harrises myself, but pushed that thought away, remembering Anne's reception.

I thought about joining the feminist group that met Wednesday nights in Gloucester, but I put the decision off because I knew how nervous and ill at ease I would be walking into a room full of strangers. Although I reminded myself that they were my sisters, I didn't feel close enough to the thought to dispel my fears. Well, I'll see, I kept telling myself, it isn't Wednesday yet.

And then of course eventually it was, and I woke up that morning, conscious of being grateful for another noiseless night, and aware that I was going to have to make a decision about going to that meeting.

Damn, I thought, why had I had to read about it anyhow? I sulked through the morning, angry at my own yellow belly. I hadn't even bothered to get dressed. It was raining and I felt slovenly.

I watched a few game shows on TV, making myself feel even more debauched, and then got up and snapped the set off angrily. "So, go!" I shouted aloud to the quiet den. And I answered myself: "All right, I will!" I knew that I would need to prod myself some. I was getting too used to my own company, and it could be that for this whole year I would talk to no one but Peabody and Mrs. Collins; appeasing myself by writing to Anne and receiving her letters — believing that was all the communication I needed.

Not healthy, I thought, going into the kitchen for some coffee, much too hermit-like.

Then I swung open the kitchen door and screamed. Outside, smashed against the window over the sink, a distorted face was staring straight at me.

I backed off, still crying out, and the face came away from the window, regaining its natural proportions. I tremblingly realized that it was because the man's face had been pressed so tightly to the glass that I had gotten the impression of distortion, disfigurement.

He raised a hand and motioned me over, pointing to the back door.

"What," I called from my end of the kitchen, "what do you want?"

He mumbled something, and inadvertently I took a step closer.

"I'm yer neighbor," he called out to me, "Paul Harris," he jerked his head around, "from nex' door."

I went stumbling quickly to the door and opened it so that the back screen still remained between us.

"Wh . . . why were you looking in my window?" I stammered, very aware of my thin robe and messy hair.

"Wasn't *looking*," he underlined, pronouncing his words carefully, "I was knockin', only you didn' hear me."

"Oh," was all I could think to say.

"Kin I come in?" he asked.

I wondered desperately for a moment whether he could, or why he even should.

And then he explained. "Jus' wanted to come over and see ya. My little Kate told me you took her cat. I seen ya out in the garden the other day, so I jus' thought I'd come over and introduce myself."

I guessed that was all right. Besides I didn't feel I could be impolite and say no to him. After all he had made a friendly gesture. But as I thought this, the word "friendly" caught in my mind. There just wasn't anything very friendly about the scruffy, sloppy-looking man standing on my back doorstep. And then I realized that I must look pretty awful to him too.

I unsnapped the lock on the screen door and held it open for him. "Come in," I said as pleasantly as I could. "I was just going to have some coffee. Why don't you pour yourself a cup and I'll be right back."

Without waiting for him to answer, I dashed out of the kitchen and upstairs, where I quickly pulled on a pair of jeans and a shirt and combed my hair. When I left my bedroom I closed the door behind me, leaving Peabody asleep on my pillow. I didn't think Mr. Harris would much appreciate having him downstairs.

But when I got back to the kitchen, feeling a little more comfortable and presentable, Mr. Harris wasn't there.

Fear immediately shot through me. Why had I let that man into the house? Maybe he wasn't my neighbor at all. Just some derelict who said he was so he could get in and — an icy fear slipped up my back and my head began to tingle in a way that made me think I was going to faint.

A sentence kept buzzing senselessly around in my mind and finally broke through to me: You've got to get out of here! Fast! Suddenly I propelled into action and shot for the back door, my slippery fingers fumbling with the knob just as I heard a sound in back of me.

An unpleasant laugh, and then Mr. Harris' voice saying, "Thought I'd gone away did you?"

I whirled around. "What? Where . . . where were you?" I asked him, knowing that he could see my fear and somehow feeling that he was not displeased by it.

"Right here," he grinned at me. "I been right here."

"No you haven't," I said and turned to the stove. Keep your hands busy doing something and your eyes away from him, I told myself.

"Just looking around a little," he said, and I was uncomfortably aware that his voice was growing nearer, that he was standing right in back of me.

"Well, you shouldn't have done that," I told him, cursing myself for being so ineffectual, and trying to pour coffee with an unsteady hand.

"Now, now," he said, patting me on the shoulder. I jerked quickly away and in doing so spilled boiling coffee all over my wrist.

"Look what you've done!" he grabbed my hand before I could stop him and thrust it under running water in the sink.

"Please," I said, rescuing my hand and pulling away from him, "I'm all right." But of course I wasn't. My hand stung terribly and was beginning to redden.

Mr. Harris just shrugged and turned away. "Suit yerself," he said, "but cold water's the best thing for a burn."

"Why don't you get yourself some coffee and I'll ... I will put some water on this," I told him, a little ashamed of my immediate reaction to his touch.

He shook his head and lurched closer to me again. "I don't want no coffee, don' you have somethin' stronger?" he asked. And then I was aware of a peculiar odor about him. Later I was amazed that I hadn't noticed it sooner, that I hadn't been aware from his first words how drunk he was.

"No," I said coldly, "just coffee."

"Don't want none of that," he said, hanging his head and letting it swing from side to side.

"Then maybe you'd better leave," I answered stiffly, inwardly pleased at myself for taking a firm stand.

"Now why you bein' so unfriendly?" he asked, reaching out an arm as if to touch me again.

I moved away from him easily and stood behind the table, resting my aching hand gingerly on a chair top. "Go home, Mr Harris."

"Well, if that's how you wanna be," he sneered. But he took a hesitant step in my direction.

"That's how," I said, keeping my voice quiet. I wasn't afraid of this man any longer. He was just drunk and obscene and I felt confident that if I gave him a shove he'd fall down immediately and have a lot of trouble getting up.

He stopped where he was, but made no move to leave.

"I don't want to have to call your wife, Mr. Harris, but you're giving me no — "

I broke off as he lunged toward me and grasped my burning wrist with more strength and power than I would have believed him to have in his condition. He wrenched my arm and I gasped in pain.

"Jus' don' you fool aroun' with me, girlie," he warned, and then, as quickly as it had happened, he released me and stalked unsteadily to the back door.

My heart pounded against my chest and

I closed my eyes and shuddered with the pain that was shooting up my arm. I could see multicolored whirling circles against my eyelids as I groped for the chair and sat down.

When I opened my eyes he was gone, as I'd been pretty sure he would be. I sat cradling my arm in my hand, shocked into disbelief over what had just happened. A few minutes later I made myself get up and lock the back doors, screen and inside. Then I walked over to the sink and ran some icy water on my arm and wrist, staring dully out the window, looking for Paul Harris' retreating back. But he'd be long gone by now, I supposed.

When my arm grew numb I turned the water off and wrapped a soft dish cloth over the swelling. But the numbness wore off quickly, and the pain started again. I went to the refrigerator and got out some ice to wrap in the cloth.

I was still deeply shocked and couldn't seem to think straight. Should I call the police? And if I did, what would I tell them? I was very new in town. I had answered my back door dressed in a skimpy robe and let a man in to have coffee with me. Then he had twisted my arm. Why, they would want to know, had he done that? And I would say I didn't know, but that he'd been drinking heavily before he came over. Then they

50

would ask me why I had allowed him to come in if I knew he was drunk, and I would have to admit that I hadn't realized he was drunk when I'd let him in. And then, I could almost see it, they would look at me, disbelieving, and I would fumble for words, try to explain. . . . I shook my head uselessly. No, this was no story to tell to the police.

Maybe Mrs. Harris then? I wondered. Should I appeal to her? But I would probably get the same reaction there. Why did you let a drunk man into your house when you weren't even properly dressed? If I told Mrs. Harris, she'd probably tell her husband, which would only make him . . . I shivered, not wanting or needing to complete that thought.

So there was nothing for me to do but lock all my doors and windows and only go out in the daytime because I was scared silly of my neighbor. Or maybe I should write to Anne and Raymond, tell them . . . but no, that would never work. They were in Europe, they'd left me with their house and had expected me to be able to cope. Well, I'd really made a terrific start at that, I laughed feebly.

The day wore on and darkened and I was still sitting at the kitchen table with my sore arm and sick fears. It was Peabody, mewing pitifully from my room, that finally made me get up and move about.

"Poor love, you want your dinner, don't you?" I told him apologetically. But I wasn't going to get around Peabody so easily. He disdainfully marched out of my bedroom and down the stairs, waving his plume of a tail and not giving me a backward glance.

Well, that takes care of the Cape Ann feminists for tonight, I thought. I'm not going to put myself through anything else today.

That night I watched television till midnight. I didn't even bother to change stations. One program followed another and I got involved in them all just so that I wouldn't have to think. And then, shortly after Johnny Carson's monologue, my eyelids began to grow heavy and I believed maybe I would be able to fall asleep. I thought tiredly about staying where I was with the television on and falling asleep on the couch, drowsing through The Mighty Carson Art Players and the female vocalist. But I decided I'd better not do that. If I kept giving in and sleeping in the den, I would start being afraid of the whole house, the creaking, settling noises it made at night, the wind dragging through the trees, a faucet dripping.

No, I told myself decisively. I have to live next door to that rotter, but I don't have to let fear of him creep in through every crevice. I'd behave sensibly, and if I had any more trouble with him I would go directly to the police.

I climbed the stairs wearily, followed by Peabody, who had finally forgiven me. As I went to close the curtains in my room, a habit I'd gotten into, I looked over at the Harris' house and was surprised to see that there were still lights on downstairs and in one of the upstairs rooms. Usually when I went to bed, certainly earlier than this, the house was in darkness. And then, as I stood there watching, I heard a car starting up and could see headlights flash across their house. The front door opened and Mrs. Harris came out and ran across their small space of lawn to the car. I noticed absently that she was very bundled up for this time of year, and then she was getting into the car. Almost before she had the door closed behind her, the car rattled off down the driveway and turned into the road that connected our houses. I stood there looking out for a while longer, but the lights in the house stayed on and I couldn't see any other movement. Kate must be in there, I thought, drawing the curtains and getting into bed, unless she was in the car too. But it didn't seem reasonable that her parents would let her go out so late on a school night.

Yet would they just leave her and the

baby there alone, I wondered, and where were *they* going so late at night? Probably to some bar, if there's one open, I thought, and was surprised by the small spasm of fear that ran through me.

If Mr. Harris weren't home, then he couldn't come prowling around here. But what about later, when he got home? What would he do then? I asked myself.

CHAPTER
FIVE

I was awakened the next morning by the insistent hammering of the front-door knocker.

I noticed dimly that it was nine o'clock and wondered why I had slept so late. As I was pulling on a pair of slippers to go down and answer the knock, I suddenly felt afraid.

Was that Mr. Harris, back to torture me again? I felt my heart begin a steady pounding that matched the raps at the door.

I went down the stairs quietly. Maybe he'd think no one was home and go away.

When I got to the front hall, I carefully parted the curtains on one of the side windows flanking the door, and peeked out.

I let out my breath when I saw who was standing there. It was only a woman! No bogey man come to get me. I walked quickly to the door and opened it wide.

"Miss ... Sohier, is it?" the woman asked me, and as she spoke I realized she looked familiar. Grizzled blonde hair made fuzzy by a permanent and large blue eyes that I thought looked fearfully at me.

I smiled. "You're Mrs. Harris, aren't you?" I asked.

"How did you know that?" She glanced uneasily about her and her wariness struck me because it was so much like Kate's.

"I saw you out on the lawn one day. You were sitting with your son. In fact it was the same day that Kate — "

"Could I come in please?" she interrupted, and I moved back to let her enter.

"I'm sorry. Of course," I said, thinking that I seemed fated to meet the Harrises in my nightclothes.

"Did I wake you up?" she asked.

"Oh, no," I assured her, feeling guilty about being found out. "I was just about to get dressed, but why don't you come and have some coffee with me first?"

"If it wouldn't be any trouble." She followed me into the kitchen, and I was again struck by the similarity of coffee, kitchen, and a Harris.

"Your daughter Kate is such a nice girl,"

I chatted, trying hard to think of something to say that would make Mrs. Harris less nervous. She was fidgeting with her hands and looked as if she were afraid to sit down.

But at my words she smiled, and a tender look came over her face. "Thank you," she said simply. "I think she is too."

I poured us each a cup of coffee and put out a plate filled with Danishes, realizing that these actions were making me feel very suburban and homelike.

"Oh, I couldn't eat anything," Mrs. Harris said, "but thank you."

I could see why she couldn't eat; she kept wetting her lips as if they were parched and giving me fearful looks, almost asking that I guess what was wrong and put her at ease. I suppose it was stupid of me not to have realized why she'd come over, but I didn't.

"Is something bothering you, Mrs. Harris?" I asked as gently as I could.

"Yes," she said in a low, almost inaudible voice. "I came over to tell you how sorry . . . to apologize. . . ."

I looked at her, uncomprehending. "For what?"

"For my husband," she responded, making me hear bells and whistles and curse myself for being such a fool.

"Oh. He told you about yesterday then?"

I sometimes discovered quite a knack in myself for asking the obvious. I probably did it most times as I was doing it now, because it gave me time to think and recover from a feeling of inadequacy.

"Well, I saw him leave here," she replied grimly, "and I could see he'd really been at it. I don't know as he told me what really happened; doubt he much remembered it by the time he got home. Anyhow, I knew it couldn't've been pleasant for you, so I come over to tell you I'm sorry for your bother."

This had been quite a long speech for her, but during it some of her nervousness had vanished and she seemed almost pleased with herself. I guessed it had not been easy to make herself come over and speak to me.

Well, I thought, if Paul Harris hadn't told her what happened, I certainly wasn't going to. And if he had really forgotten about it, that made me breathe easier too.

"It's all right, Mrs. Harris. I think probably your husband just meant to be neighborly." Oh, Tanya, why are you saying that, my mind screamed at me, and made me add, "Although it didn't turn out quite that way." I paused. "Probably because, as you said, he'd been drinking."

Mrs. Harris nodded at me and started to get up.

"Oh, you're not going yet, are you?" I

asked her, alarmed. Even if her husband was a rat there was no reason why she and I couldn't be friendly I was growing tired of the sound of my own voice talking to Peabody and, sometimes, even just to myself. "You haven't touched your coffee yet," I tried.

"I can't stay," she said, edging away from me and becoming jittery again. She seemed very eager to leave.

"That's too bad," I told her, amazed at how disappointed I was and how much I obviously needed a little companionship. Most any other time I would have crossed the street to avoid a Mrs. Harris, who was rather slovenly looking and didn't seem to be terribly bright.

"Maybe you'll stop over another time," I told her, and she mumbled something back at me that I didn't catch.

"Please tell Kate that Peabody is fine," I said, "and that she can come over and visit him whenever she likes."

"Peabody?" Mrs. Harris turned to face me. We were standing at the front door.

"Yes, the cat. She did tell you — "

"Oh, sure. I knew she'd given him to you. I just didn't know she'd given him a name, that's all."

And I wonder whether you know how much she cared about him too, I asked her silently. But that was probably unfair of me, I thought, remembering Mrs. Harris' face when Kate's name had been mentioned.

"I haven't seen your little one outside lately," I said, detaining her and wondering vaguely why I was bothering to try.

"It's the weather, been too nippy, and he's got a bit of a cold," she answered quickly. "Well, I'll be leaving now. Thank you, Miss Sohier. I'm glad things wasn't worse with Paul."

She was out the door and down the path before I could answer. That whole house is nutty, I thought, going upstairs to dress.

But not Kate, I amended, nothing wrong there.

As I was making my bed, it occurred to me to wonder how much "worse" Paul might have been. I shivered. He'd been quite bad enough, thank you! But then, of course, his wife didn't know that. Or did she guess?

That afternoon I wrote Anne and Raymond a long chatty letter, mostly about what I knew and didn't know about their neighbors. I edited out the scene with Paul Harris, saying only that we'd met briefly outside and that I quite concurred with Anne's opinion. It made me feel good to write the letter, at least it was a way of reaching out and communicating with someone. And who nicer to talk to, I thought, immediately feeling a sharp stab of disappointment that Anne wasn't here right now so I could really tell her everything that had been going on.

The next week was delightful. No more strange faces plastered at my windows; lovely, blissful, noiseless nights with only the sound of crickets murmuring outside; and gentle winds coming up from the river. And then the realization that an Indian summer was settling onto Cape Ann.

There were mellow days ending in splendid streaky sunsets; the leaves stayed on the trees, holding their vibrant color in the warm sunlight as if the bitterness of autumn would never reach them.

I spent most of my mornings out of doors, gardening and reading, and rejoicing in the thick changing colors. It was like living inside a ripe melon.

During the longish afternoons I discovered a passion for rock climbing. I drove all over the Cape, stopping wherever I found a wall of rocks leading out to the sea. After a few days of clutching and clawing along on my hands and knees, and feeling swimmy when I got to a high point forming a precipice to the sea, I finally grew braver and more nimble. Abandoning my crouch-climb, I could now leap agilely from one rock to another.

I became friendly with the sea and delighted in the heather and thistles which sprung up from between the rocks. Afternoons I would return to the house, my arms filled with heather and sea oats, and scavenge about for every vase, bucket, or bowl I could find.

Soon the rooms were glowing with deep pink and brown shades that made them a pleasure to walk into and rediscover the foaming flowers and stark, intricately patterned branches.

It was on one of these days, when I got home later than usual, that I next saw Paul Harris.

I was just getting out of the car, my arms laden with milk-pod weeds that I'd unexpectedly discovered growing along the roadside, when I heard a scream, followed by the sound of a man cursing.

I dropped the pods and ran around to the side of the house in time to see Peabody limping toward me, followed by Mr. Harris who was of course doing the cursing, while waving a mean-looking stick about in the air.

"Peabody!" I wailed and darted forward to pick up my kitten, who huddled in my arms, shaking and whimpering.

"What have you done?" I screamed at the man. "What have you *done* to him!"

"You keep your damn cat away from my house, lady," he yelled back, his face red with anger. "I hate the lousy things, they give me the creeps," he said, lowering his stick, but still looking mean enough to use it again, on Peabody or me.

But this time I wasn't retreating. "What's the *matter* with you?" I demanded, furious and near crying. "It's only a little kitten!" I pressed Peabody closer to me, but he squirmed and cried out in pain so that I had to loosen my hold on him.

"He wuz pokin' around in my garage and I give him a good kick. That's what I done, and that's what I'll do again if I ever catch him around here!"

I turned away wordlessly. That was no man over there, that was an animal. I was crying freely now, both from frustration and fear that Peabody was hurt badly. As I carried him into the house, I wondered briefly how he had managed to get out. Hadn't I locked everything up before I'd left? And then I remembered the den window, the one without a screen that I'd left open to air the house.

I began to castigate myself for being so stupid and then I let it all go as useless. The important thing now was to get Peabody to a vet. I hurriedly pulled a blanket from the linen closet and tucked it around the little shivery body. Then I fumbled through the Gloucester directory, first looking up doctors and then realizing that the name I needed would be listed under veterinarians.

There was one in Gloucester, a Dr. David Montserrat. When I read the name I remembered that of course I had known that all along. I'd frequently passed his house, with a shingle hanging outside it, when I drove into town.

I quickly scooped Peabody up and rushed from the house. But I made myself drive slowly and carefully toward town. It had rained this morning, and I was taking no chances of skidding on wet leaves and catapulting us both into the ocean.

Finally I saw it — a white house on the right with the sign I had remembered outside. I felt a shaky sense of relief as I turned into the driveway and parked. Here Peabody and I were, safely in front of the doctor's house without having been pursued. I realized then that ever since I had turned away from Paul Harris and taken Peabody into the house, I'd definitely felt as if I were being chased, or at the very least that some dark, impenetrable cloud was slowly lowering on me.

Carrying Peabody, I approached the front door with a twinge of misgiving. Should I have called first? I looked at my watch and saw that it was after five. Did vets have office hours the way other doctors did? I supposed that they must, but this did, after all, look like a regular house. So Dr. Montserrat probably lived here, and if he did, then hopefully he was at home.

I knocked hesitantly, hating the shyness and fear that were becoming mixed up inside me.

I heard footsteps coming to the door and then a voice asking, "Yes? Who is it?"

"I . . . it's my kitten. Could you help me?" I replied hesitantly.

The door opened and a tall thin man with dark hair stood before me. "I don't have office hours on Wednesdays," he began, and then stopped when he heard Peabody's whines.

He stood back to let me enter and I began babbling at him, "I'm sorry to have to bother you, Dr. Montserrat, but he's hurt and I didn't know what to do. I've just had him a few weeks and I don't know too much about animals. I — "

But the doctor was reaching for the bundle that was Peabody as if he hadn't heard me. I quickly closed my mouth and stood watching him probe about inside the blanket.

"Let's go back to my office," he said, and I followed him through a waiting hall and into a small examining room, where he switched on a glaring overhead light and placed Peabody on a stark metal table.

The next ten minutes or so were agonizing. Dr. Montserrat worked quietly, pausing only once to ask me how this had happened.

"A neighbor," I replied briefly. "My kitten wandered onto his property and he kicked him."

I couldn't see his reaction to this because his back was turned to me, but as I repeated to him what had happened, the whole scene with that odious man came back to me and made me begin to shake almost as badly as the kitten.

Finally the doctor again covered Peabody with the blanket and turned to me. I noticed that his hair was finely shot with gray and that he had a craggy face that looked homey.

He put his hands deep into his slacks pockets and seemed so at ease and relaxed that I felt my breathing slow. When he smiled, I smiled wobbly back at him. Then it was going to be all right, wasn't it? Peabody would be fine? I was afraid to ask. It was nice just to bathe for a moment in this hope.

"You did just the right thing, of course, keeping him warm and bringing him right here," Dr. Montserrat said.

"What . . . what's wrong with him?" I managed.

"He has either a sprain or a broken leg. I won't be sure till I can X-ray it, and I'm afraid that will have to wait till tomorrow when I can take him over to the hospital. Unless it's a real emergency, the technicians don't like to open up shop again after five."

"Oh," I said in a small voice, and then, "Is he . . . will he be all right?"

"I'm sure he will," the doctor replied, and then his face grew serious. "You say your neighbor kicked him?" he asked me, and when I nodded, not trusting my voice, he just shook his head, and muttered, "People are really incredible."

"Yes," I said, thinking he didn't begin to know how much so. "Do you want me to leave Peabody with you till tomorrow then?" I asked him.

"Peabody?" he grinned.

"Yes. That's what the little girl who gave him to me had already named him. But I rather like it," I added, deciding not to tell him who the "little girl's" father was. Everything was disturbing enough as it was without going through a whole series of explanations.

"Peabody," Dr. Montserrat repeated and reached over to stroke the blanket, clumsily but gently. "Fine name," he said, and then, "Yes, I do think you should leave him here with me till tomorrow. He's in shock now, and I've put a temporary splint on the leg, but I'm anxious to see what the X rays show."

I began to feel all quaky inside again, and Dr. Montserrat seemed to notice it. "Here," he said, coming toward me. "He'll be fine where he is for the moment. I've given him an injection to make him sleep. Why don't you come inside and sit down?" He looked at me. "You're paler and more frightened than he is now," he accused sternly, and I was suddenly glad for his hand propelling me through another door and into what was obviously his living room. Through a slight haze I was aware of earth colors — tans and browns and oranges. He pushed slightly against my shoulder and I obediently sank down into a soft velvety-feeling couch.

I was aware of Dr. Montserrat standing above me, saying, "I certainly didn't mean to alarm you, Mrs. — "

"Sohier," I answered automatically. "Miss. Tanya Sohier," I said, looking up and feeling an unexpected burst of delight at just looking at Dr. Montserrat. Now where was that coming from? I puzzled.

"Do you live on Cape Ann, Miss Sohier?"

"Yes . . . well, no, not exactly. That is, I live here for this year anyway. I'm taking care of someone's house, the Rinns, while they're away in Europe. I was a little lonely at first, that's why it's been so nice to have Peabody," I rattled on, wondering wildly if I were about to give him my birth-

68

date and favorite color next. How in the midst of this could I find him so attractive? I stopped talking abruptly and got up.

"I'm all right now," I said, "and I think I've taken enough of your time." I could hear myself sounding very prim and waspish.

"Not at all, Miss Sohier. I'm glad to have been here." He seemed amused by something.

I made a tentative move toward the door, realizing how much I didn't want to go back to the Rinns', and terribly tempted to tell Dr. Montserrat the whole elliptical story. But of course that would have been ridiculous.

"Shall I call you tomorrow? About picking Peabody up I mean," I said and reddened. What had I thought he would think I meant?

"Fine. Anytime after two," he replied, walking me to the door. I wondered fleetingly if he were on his way out. If he had a date with someone and I was holding him back. Or maybe he was married? And what did it matter if he was? I asked myself angrily. What had it to do with me?

I turned at the door and made myself smile. "Thank you," I told him, "I'll see you tomorrow." And with that promise to both of us, I quickly walked to my car.

CHAPTER
SIX

I felt very skittish and unsure of myself on the way home. The memory of the look on Mr. Harris' face began to attack me, but it got mixed up with the pleasant, uncluttered face of Dr. Montserrat. And just as fear was welling up in me for the one, I felt my face cover with funny, quirky smiles as I recalled the other. Then concern for Peabody blotted out both images, and I drove slowly toward the Rinns', overcome suddenly by depression.

As I got out of the car, I stepped on something crunchy that made me jump and cry out in fear. Then from the light in the car I could see my forgotten milk pods scattered over the driveway. Tears stung my eyes as I recalled how happy and un-threatened I'd been a few hours ago.

I gathered up the pods and turned to go into the house, my eyes flickering over to the Harris' for a moment. Their house was lit up cozily for nighttime — it looked like just any wood-frame country house, nestled in the trees.

That night I slept in my own bed, being too tired and low for a retreat to the den with the television yammering at me all night. Besides, my exhaustion replaced any fear that might threaten to creep up on me.

Paul Harris had done all he was going to do for one day. And as I fell off to sleep I was lulled by a curious sense of safety that must have arisen from the snaps of David Montserrat that kept shooting off in my sleepy mind.

I dressed carefully to go and pick up Peabody the next day. I was sure I had looked a mess the day before and I was eager that David (David?) should see me differently.

You know you shouldn't be doing this, I rebuked myself, choosing a pair of soft tan slacks and a lemony sweater, you're just doing the conventional man-woman role thing. If you look pretty, he'll like you. That sort of junk.

But today I didn't much care about principles. A hangover from the depression I'd suffered the night before was still with me, and I was feeling sorry enough for myself to need to at least look attractive and assured *outside*.

I'd called David and though he'd told me that Peabody did indeed have a broken leg, he also said that it was a clean, simple break, nothing for me to be concerned about, and that he would plaster up the leg and I could come for Peabody around three.

I put on my new suede jacket, tied a gypsy colored scarf around my neck, and left the house at three fifteen. I drove slowly, not because of the weather, it was a golden day with high blue clouds, but because I would not arrive panting on his doorstep at three exactly. No need at all for him to know that despite how ugly I was feeling today, I was terribly eager to see him again.

It's probably because it's the first friendly adult face you've seen in weeks, I tried letting myself down — gently, so I wouldn't hurt too much. But I knew that it must be more than that. I wasn't yet so desperate that I could become involved by just a friendly face.

When I got to David's house I noticed that his visiting hours were posted on the front door, and saw that I was arriving just as they would be over. Had he planned that? When he answered my knock I could tell that he was not displeased to see me.

"Hello, Dr. Montserrat."

"Miss Sohier," he smiled. "You're looking a lot less peaked today."

"I'm feeling it," I lied, following him into the house, and surprised when he led me into the living room instead of his examining room.

"I've got Peabody all fixed up for you," he said. "Why don't you wait in here and I'll bring him in."

As I sat down on the same couch I'd been quivering and shaking on yesterday, I realized with a start that I hadn't even thought about paying him. I supposed I should have already offered.

"Here he is," David said, coming through the door with a woefully trussed up Peabody in his arms.

"Oh, sweetie," I rushed over and took my kitten from him. "What a lot you've been through!" I nuzzled the soft little head to my neck and heard Peabody begin his low, growling purr.

I turned to David. "I've just realized that I didn't think about paying you yesterday," I apologized.

"No problem," he said. "Besides, I had Peabody for ransom."

I bent to put the kitten on the rug. "Is it all right if he walks around?"

"Of course. Just keep him as quiet as possible until the leg heals. Better keep him indoors from now on too. Cats don't really mind that, and then you won't have to worry about him being hit by a car, or," he added grimly, "coming into contact with your neighbor's foot again."

"Yes, I will do that," I told him, not bothering to explain that Peabody had gotten out through my own carelessness.

"It mustn't be very pleasant for you, living next door to a man who kicks cats," he sympathized.

"No, of course it isn't," I replied in a low voice, shaking my head and letting my hair swing away from my face. You're shameless, Tanya, I grinned inwardly. "I can't say I'm exactly fond of that man."

"Well," he seemed hesitant, and I knew that as soon as he told me his fee I would have to leave. Maybe I could offer to be his receptionist or something, I thought wildly. "How long have you been at the —Rinns', did you say it was? Miss Sohier?"

"Only a few weeks, *Dr.* Montserrat," I said, bravely underscoring the doctor part. I took a breath. "Tanya would be easier," I said smiling at him as a last-ditch lure. In a few moments I was going to find myself out of here with nothing positive having happened between us.

"Tanya, then," he laughed, "and I suppose I shall have to let you call me David."

I wondered why I kept having the feeling that he was amused by me.

"Well, you don't need to force yourself," I replied tartly, suddenly feeling prickly and vulnerable.

He grimaced. "I guess I can handle it all right." His eyes twinkled at me and again I felt that I had evoked his laughter.

Well, I thought, getting up, I guess it's time to go now. At least we're on a first-name basis. For whatever that's worth. I'd tried flirting with the man and he'd laughed at me. It was infuriating, but maybe not so very surprising since I'd never tried being cute with anyone before.

And don't forget, if you ever decide to try again, how unsuccessful it was, I told myself, reaching down to untangle Peabody from David's shaggy rug.

"Are you in a rush?" he asked.

I decided, against the first swell of pleasure at his words, that I ought to be. "I am really," I told him, hoping that I wasn't pushing things too far, that I would come up against some opposition.

"I suppose house-sitting isn't a twenty-four hour occupation, is it?" David asked.

"Not quite. I manage a few hours a day to myself," I said.

"Then how about spending those hours with me this Sunday?" he proposed, and

I felt a kind of happiness I'd never experienced before well up in me.

"I'd like that," I told him simply.

"And so would I," David replied.

After paying and giving him directions to the Rinns', I left, slowly, smilingly, with Peabody tucked under my arm.

As I drove home I sang and waved happily to a gull screaming away above the car. I felt, just then, extremely good and marvelously alive.

The next few days were halcyon: sun-warmed, and still glittering with autumn color. Pumpkins flourished on doorsteps, and cutouts of witches, scarecrows, and cats decorated the windows of houses. I realized that Halloween was not far off and planned to buy some corn to pop for any trick or treaters who came by. Our road wasn't well traveled, but surely in the country I would be besieged by goblins and ghosts and all sorts of rubber-masked horrors.

I had succeeded in pushing any thoughts of the Harrises far from my mind, and was just beginning to convince myself that if neither Peabody nor I encroached on their territory, they'd leave us alone too. At least I fervently hoped they would.

On Saturday morning a long letter came from Anne. I grasped it eagerly and went outside to savor it. It was a warm, humorous letter, filled with all the faux pas Anne had managed to make at a formal London dinner party they'd attended. I read the letter over twice, smiling at the pictures Anne's words formed.

And then, just as I was about to go back inside, I was stopped by the sound of crying. I looked around me quickly, thinking that maybe Peabody had wandered out with me and was stuck somewhere. But I didn't see him, and as I listened I realized the crying was much more human than animal.

Except for that noise, it was very quiet out. For once no wind, or even a slight breeze, was coming from the river. And there wasn't the usual early Saturday afternoon sounds of cheering from the Gloucester high school, which often reached me when they were having a football game. Just that crying, going on as if it would never stop.

I walked around the lawn, trying to detect the direction the sound was coming from. I suppose I only did that out of a vague hope that it might be some child in the road who had fallen off a bicycle, something like that, and that I wouldn't find that the sounds were coming from the direction of the Harris' house.

I ended up on the side lawn, staring

over at my neighbors, and hearing that sad, piteous noise very clearly now. There could be no mistaking the direction from which it was coming.

I stood unmoving, listening. It couldn't be Kate, could it? The cries sounded more as if they were coming from a much younger child. Her brother? I was riveted to that one spot on the lawn, not knowing what to do.

I saw that Mr. Harris' car was parked in front of the house, so presumably someone was home and could hear the crying much better than I could out here. Then why didn't they do something about it? I asked myself in a spasm of nerves and fear. How could they just let a baby go on crying like that?

And then, as quickly as the sound had begun, it stopped. Almost as if a pillow had been put over the child's head to make it stop, I thought involuntarily, and jumped at the ugly picture I had conjured.

I waited a full five minutes, and then, hearing nothing else, turned and walked back to the house, trying to puzzle it out.

Well, it's none of your business anyhow, I told myself, slamming the front door hard behind me to break the sudden stillness in the air.

Should I perhaps call them, I wondered, just to see if everything was all right?

But if I did that they would only think I was being nosy and would probably be rude to me. No, I would do nothing at all, I decided, irritated that yet something more to disquiet me had come from that horrid household.

And where had Kate gone? I wondered, walking through the house, too jittery to sit or do anything else. I had only seen her that one time with Peabody. What had they done, sold her into white slavery?

The afternoon passed uneasily for me, and it was after five before I remembered that I had planned to wash my hair and dry it out in the sun so it would be all floaty and lovely for tomorrow. I had also planned to do a lot of other things to straighten out my uneven appearance before Sunday, but all of them had been forgotten too.

Those people are really getting to me, I thought, finally selecting another one of Raymond's inexhaustible supply of mysteries, and trying to settle down to read.

It worked for a few chapters, and then I was up and pacing again. The day really was a waste, I thought, finally deciding to just wash my hair, blow it dry, and go to bed. Whatever David found on Sunday would just have to be all right.

That night, as I was putting on my pajamas, I started to feel very disheartened about the next day. I was struck with the terrible thought that I had somehow coerced David to ask me out. I *had* just hung about his home when I should have paid him, thanked him, and left. He probably hadn't known what to do to get rid of me. He probably thought I was young and silly, and had felt sorry for me being cloistered in a house by myself for a whole year, and wanted to do something kind. Sunday dinner with David, if he even got around to offering me a meal, would most likely be a quickie at McDonald's, I thought, torturing myself. Why had I believed I could attract him? Old Tanya Sohier who'd only been on about six dates in her whole life, and all of those unsuccessful.

It was the crying and the Harrises that had started all my glooming, and now I was rushed out of the soft, pleasant days I'd spent since David had asked me out, straight into the chill, gray weather where I usually lived.

CHAPTER
SEVEN

Sunday morning was hunched in clouds, and a fine rain had begun to fall. I breathed a martyr's sigh. Naturally. The weather was only a foreshadowing of the day ahead of me, I thought nastily, seeing the morning stretch endlessly before me.

As I sat at the kitchen table, drinking my coffee black because I'd forgotten to go to the store for milk, I thought that I ought to use this morning to do something industrious. Make it pass, anyhow, till two when David was to come for me. I'd weed, I decided. The earth would be nice and soft, making it easier for me. I'd been putting off weeding for a week, and I would do it now, as a penance for having lost all of yesterday.

When I got outside, I realized what a mess the damp weather was going to make of my hair. By this afternoon it would be straight and straggly. Oh, who cares, I thought, viciously attacking a spiny-looking thing that was growing a foot up out of the zinnias.

I worked hard for over an hour, thinking of nothing but what I was doing, and deriving some satisfaction from seeing how trim and neat the flower beds were beginning to look. After a little longer I decided I'd had enough, and sat back in the coolish wet grass to relax and admire my work.

Not bad at all, Tanya, I was congratulating myself, as I saw the side door of the Harris house open. I pushed myself forward a little and peered through the gloomy day to see who was coming out. I was mostly hidden by a clipped evergreen, and that made me feel safe. It was Mr. Harris I saw, and I certainly didn't want him to think I was spying. Which of course I was.

I watched as he dragged a long ladder from the garage and propped it up against the house. Probably just doing some repairs, I shrugged, and began to collect my weed basket and tools, wondering for a moment why he would pick a day like this. Goes along with his creepy disposition, I told myself, standing up to stretch and get the kinks out of my back and legs.

The steady rapping of a hammer on wood made me turn around to see what he was doing. It also made me drop the small trowel I'd been holding in my hand. Mr. Harris was boarding up the windows on the second story of his house. He had a number of thick wide boards resting on a ledge beside his ladder, and he was methodically nailing them into place so that they totally obscured his upper windows.

Was he closing up the house for the winter? Were they going away? I wondered, tasting joy. Oh, what a relief that would be! I stood watching him work for a few moments, feeling a weight come sliding down off me, and experiencing such a deep delight that I realized just how heavily the Harrises had been oppressing me.

I turned away happily. Mr. Harris could easily manage without me watching him, and it was getting late.

As I dressed for David, I kept convincing myself, against a slight feather of doubt that had begun to tickle at me, that the Harrises were indeed moving away — at least for winter. Weeks ago I had driven along the shore and beach roads on the Cape and watched people do exactly what he was doing now — closing up their houses before the snow began.

The only hitch I could see in the Harrises doing the same thing was that they didn't

look financially capable of wintering somewhere, and spending spring and summer
in Gloucester.

Why did I have to think of that? I asked
myself, mussing my hair up on my head to
try and give it some badly needed body.
Maybe one of them had a mother or father
somewhere that they would be spending
the winter with. A slim hope, I guessed, but
one I planned to cherish for as long as
possible.

David was prompt, which I had figured
on. What I had not expected, what hadn't
even dimly passed through my mind, was
that he didn't seem at all happy — in fact
what he looked was quite uncomfortable
when I opened the door to him.

Oh, dear, I thought, seeing his face. At
least I had hoped that the day would begin
a little more happily than this. Time
enough for him to get jaded during the
next five hours or so. Five hours! I quailed.

My smile was a bit trembly and uncertain as I asked him to come in.

He did step inside, but just. "You look
beautifully autumnal, Tanya," he said, but
his voice was chilly and he had no more
than glanced at my rusty wool skirt, orange
shirt, and black tights.

"Thank you," I told him in a frozen
voice, wondering if I could possibly double

over with an acute attack of appendicitis.

"Well, are you ready?" he asked.

I quickly put on my jacket and followed him out to the car, unpleasant forbodings playing tag in my stomach.

We rolled down the driveway with the uncomfortable promise of David's boredom hanging over us as heavily as the deepening clouds.

I sat way over on my side of the car, with my knees tight together and my purse in my lap, as wooden and unmoving as the little Harris boy had been in the yard that afternoon. David seemed to have nothing to say, and I cast desperately around, past the weather, and considered telling him about my gardening or rock climbing, but I gave them both up as being boring and definitely not conversation-openers. My aunt had always told me how important it was to have a conversation-opener, but till now I'd never needed one.

Then, as we turned toward the harbor, I began to get angry. Why had he asked me out anyhow if he was going to be such a sphynx? Where was that warm, smiling, teasing man I had left on Thursday? He could make an effort, after all. Couldn't he see that I was suffering? Didn't he feel any responsibility to me at all? I pressed my lips tightly together and resolved not to jabber meaninglessly at him. Let him talk, when he could think of something to say.

Suddenly David pulled up in front of the fishermen's memorial statue that guarded the harbor. He switched off the ignition and turned to face me.

"Tanya, I'm sorry," he said immediately. "I really haven't been exactly friendly since I picked you up, have I?"

I shook my head at him mutely.

"I really *am* sorry," he repeated, touching me lightly on the shoulder. "Could we start over, or are you too irritated with me?"

I mellowed at once. In fact, I was afraid that forgiveness was shooting from my eyes like comic-book stars. But I was still confused.

"It's all right, David," I reassured him, and then paused, needing to say something more. "Do you . . . can you tell me what's the matter? Or what *was* the matter?"

He withdrew a little. "I would rather not. It's nothing that concerns you, and it isn't even interesting."

"Oh," I replied, a little crestfallen. David concerned me, so why wouldn't his moods? But I didn't suppose our relationship was at a point yet where I could tell him that.

"Tanya? I thought we were just going to begin again?"

I forced a smile. "Yes, let's do that." And if I sounded less than enthusiastic, David did not seem to notice.

"Have you seen Hammond Castle yet?" he asked me, starting the engine.

"No, I haven't. Am I going to?"

"You are," he said and we sped quickly away from the harbor.

The Castle really was one — including moat, smashed bottles cemented into the tops of walls ("They used that method to guard against intruders," David enlightened me), a drawbridge, an indoor pond overgrown with vines and plants, and a great hall with a fireplace I could have walked into.

We took a tour and then walked about the grounds. The Castle was built out over the ocean, and the view of the coast was spectacular.

David pointed to an unimposing gray boulder about thirty yards out in the sea. It was covered with hundreds of sea gulls.

"Do you know what that is?" he asked me.

I shook my head. "I don't think so. A nesting ground maybe?"

"Well, now it is. It's called Norman's Woe, and is the sight of the wreck of the *Hesperus*."

"Really?" I was enchanted and stood gazing out at the rock, happy to be finding out things about Cape Ann, and feeling all warm and lovely with David next to me.

"You like all this?" His gesture took in the Castle, ocean, and gardens.

"Oh, David, it's so wonderful, it really is. You can't imagine how wonderful unless you've lived in New York." I sighed. "I'm so happy," I said without thinking.

And then David turned me around and kissed me, and I realized that I hadn't been nearly as happy a moment before as I was now. My arms went around him easily and I laid my head against his shoulder.

"I'm glad I found you, Tanya," he murmured, so low that I thought maybe I had made up the words to please myself.

Later, we sat in the great hall watching the silent version of *The Hunchback of Notre Dame*, while a huge organ above us played chilling music. I reached for David's hand, slightly amazed at my own audacity, and watched enraptured.

"It was wonderful," I told him when we were back outside, blinking in the sudden sunlight.

"Are you a horror movie buff too?" he asked.

"I certainly am," I told him, delighted. "In fact I've been almost living my own little horror show lately." That last just slipped out. I hadn't really thought whether I should mention the Harrises to David, and now that I had, I felt a chill wash over me. Besides, why put a blight on the day when they would be leaving so soon anyhow?

We were walking toward his car, but David stopped and looked at me. "What do you mean?" he questioned seriously.

"Oh, nothing," I tried to laugh, "really nothing. I was just being dramatic. Anyhow, now *I* don't want to talk about it," I teased him.

But David was not going to let me off so easily. "We'll see about that," he told me, and then, "Aren't you hungry? It's about time we had some dinner, isn't it?"

"I'm starved," I said, suddenly realizing that I hadn't eaten a thing all day.

We drove out toward the land's edge and stopped at a lovely restaurant which looked like a travel-folder ad for historic New England inns and eateries. There must have been thirty fireplaces in the old restored house (David said circa 1700), and little round niches molded into the walls where two people could eat and talk quite privately.

I felt all tawny and warm sitting across from David and sipping a glass of sherry. I was just drifting along, pleased with myself and loving the new Tanya who was emerging with so many less thorns and so much more gentleness, when David's voice cut across my reverie.

"Now what's all this about your own private horror show?"

"Oh, it's nothing, David, really. Just the people who live next door to me — the Harrises — he's the man who kicked Peabody. They've been making me a little edgy lately, that's all. But that's going to be all over with now, and I don't want to spoil today by talking about them." I rushed this all out, willing it not to be part of us.

But David was looking serious and upset. "What else has this man done besides kick Peabody?" he wanted to know.

"Oh, he scared me one day when he was drunk, that's all," I said hurriedly, hoping David would not pursue it any further.

"Tanya," he began.

But I put a stopping hand on his arm. "Please?" I asked him. "I really hate this conversation."

"Tanya, I want to know more — "

"David, stop it! Really," I said angrily.

But he just frowned at me. "Why are you so upset, then, if everything's all over now?"

I subsided, feeling crooked inside. "Sorry," I muttered, and was saved from saying anything else by a waitress hovering over us. "Let's order, David, I'm famished," I told him, relieved.

We did order, and after the waitress left us David seemed to have decided to go along with me and drop the Harrises.

I relaxed and easily managed to eat a huge meal while we talked quietly of anything and everything we could think of.

By the time David drove me home that evening I thought I knew all there was to know about him. And it had been lovely and warm and releasing to tell him about me. I'd never even had a girl friend I could talk to as easily and freely as I had to David.

We drove up to the Rinns' and David parked in the driveway, cutting his headlights. He took me in his arms and held me close. "I don't like to think of you being here all alone," he told me, and for a frantic moment I wondered if that were some kind of proposition.

"I'm not all alone," I said shakily. "I have Peabody with me, remember?"

David grunted. "A fine watch dog!"

"Oh shut up," I said, putting my lips over his, and reexperiencing that delicious sensation I'd had in the Castle gardens.

David held me tight, kissing me beautifully for a few moments before he pushed me away from him. "You're a shameless woman, Tanya Sohier," he told me, and I leaned back complacently against the car seat.

"Isn't it a beautiful night, David?" I asked.

"Honey," he told me calmly, "it's raining."

"Yes, I know," I murmured softly.

Later that evening I gently tested my feelings. What is this? I asked my fuzzy self, are you in love with the man? So soon? So quickly?

But no matter the length of time, there was no need for me to ask what I knew. A slow smile curved my lips and a new softness made me feel incandescent.

CHAPTER
EIGHT

The next day I saw Kate out on her lawn and called to her. She seemed to be collecting something on the ground, under a tree, and looked up when she heard her name shouted.

"Come on over and talk to me," I hailed her happily.

She got up, carrying a large scarf filled with something, and started toward me somewhat hesitantly.

"What have you got there?" I asked when she reached me.

"Buckeyes from the horse chestnut tree," she said, opening the scarf so that I could look.

I picked one out, holding its rounded

smoothness in my palm. "I've never seen a buckeye before," I told her in delight and surprise. But today, I thought with a tick of irony, I would go into raptures over any small thing that presented itself.

"They're all over here," Kate said without much interest.

"Why don't you come in and have a soda or something with me?" I invited.

"I have to help my mother with dinner," Kate hedged, and I wondered what about me seemed to put her off. After I'd finally gotten her to come in last time, I thought we'd both enjoyed it. But maybe that was my myth. I probably seemed ancient to Kate.

"Not even time to see Peabody and have a Pepsi and some chocolate-chip cookies I just baked?" I tried coaxing her. Perhaps she was really afraid that she'd be annoying me.

She smiled that wonderful sunny smile that did so many good things to her face. "Well ... for a few minutes," she said, "I'd like to."

It's a shame, I thought, leading the way into the house, that she's too young for me to tell about David.

Kate was delighted with Peabody. She immediately sat down on the floor and began petting him and talking to him tenderly. I moved around her, getting out glasses and putting the cookies on a plate, wondering why she wasn't asking me any questions about the kitten's leg.

I opened my mouth to say something to her, and then shut it quickly. What had I been thinking of! I couldn't say, "See poor Peabody's leg? It was your rotten father that did that to him." But why wasn't Kate asking? Had she seen the whole thing herself? No, it couldn't be that because she wouldn't have been able to watch quietly from a window while her father kicked Peabody. She loved the kitten too much to have endured that. Then had Mr. Harris told her himself? I wondered. I could just see Paul Harris holding this over Kate, to warn her against ever bringing another animal home. The pig!

Having answered my own question, I resolved not to mention the accident either. Any reference would only hurt her.

"Come sit down and talk to me," I invited, and Kate reluctantly left our kitten and sat at the table across from me.

"He's gotten so big," she said happily.

"Oh, he hasn't," I said with a laugh, "it's just that you haven't seen him for a while."

But that was the wrong thing to say. Kate's face clouded. "I've missed Peabody," she told me.

"Kate, you can come over whenever you like. Really. You don't bother me at all. In fact I'm happy to have you visit me. I hardly know anyone in Gloucester." I smiled, thinking, but now of course you do, my dear.

"Thank you," Kate said. "I *would* like to, but . . . I have to help my mother lots and . . ."

"Oh, it's okay," I quickly reassured her, seeing her embarrassment.

"I saw your father boarding up the windows," I said to change the subject. "When are you going to move?"

"Move?" Kate asked me blankly. "What do you mean? We're not moving, Tanya."

"You're . . . you're not?"

"No," Kate said, shaking her head and taking a sip of Pepsi.

"Then why was your father . . . ? I mean, I just assumed — "

"Oh." Kate seemed wary all of a sudden. "I don't know. He said it would get drafty upstairs in the winter, that's all."

"Drafty? Well, if he was worried about that, he could just . . ." But I didn't finish my sentence. After all, Kate's father's eccentricities were none of my concern. But I did feel a definite sinking in my stomach realizing that the Harrises were going to go on being my neighbors. The knowledge was even able to partially eclipse my happiness.

"How's the baby?" I asked Kate without

much interest, wanting only to change the subject.

"Oh, all right," she told me, equally uninterested.

"Your mother said he had the sniffles," I remarked idly, and Kate laughed.

"*He* did? You mean my *sister*?" she said to me, still laughing. There was high color in her cheeks, and I thought she was getting too much amusement out of my confusion.

"What do you mean, Kate?" I was sharper than I'd meant to be, but it is not pleasant to be laughed at. Especially to be laughed at indulgently, which was how I was experiencing Kate's unsuppressed nervous giggles.

"I mean I don't have a brother!" she explained, and now I really felt she was finding this situation a lot more humorous than it was. She was overreacting, I thought suddenly, wondering why.

"You told me," I said to her, my voice calm and even, "when you gave me Peabody, you told me that you had a little brother. I even saw him sitting on the lawn with your mother when you went back to the house."

"I couldn't have told you that, Tanya," Kate insisted, some laughter still in her voice, "because it's a girl my mother has, not a little boy."

"Kate, I don't talk to enough people up

here to get confused about what they tell me. . . ." I began, wondering at the same time why I was arguing with her about something so ridiculous. Kate must know better than I whether she had a brother or a sister!

"You must have misunderstood me," was all she replied, getting up and carrying her dish and glass politely to the sink.

"Why don't you come over and visit Peabody and me more often, Kate?" I said impulsively. "I'd like us to be friends."

Kate seemed startled. "You would?" she asked me.

And then it was my turn to laugh. "Of course I would."

"I . . . I would like to, if you would like to have me," she said shyly. "I'll have to ask my . . . mother, though. She needs me lots around the house. I don't have too much time usually."

Was she hedging? "Well, whenever you can and would like to," I told her. "And tell your mother I said so."

Kate smiled, and I could see the shyness was still there. "Thank you," she told me seriously. "I will."

She's a nice little person, I thought when she'd gone. I hope they treat her well! And I surprised myself by my own intense feeling. It would be easy to get attached to Kate, I realized, also knowing at once that both her parents would made that difficult for me to do. I couldn't see either one of the Harrises allowing Kate to go to Boston to a show or museum with me, or for that matter, even into town.

I shrugged, guessing that I would be lucky if her mother even allowed her to come over and visit once in awhile.

Still, I thought, sitting down to write Anne and Raymond, it was peculiar about Kate's sister/brother. I'd been so sure. Had I really misunderstood her? If I had, then I must be getting addlepated, living way up here with just the trees and the river and Peabody.

I spent the next few days wandering about happily, if somewhat aimlessly. I kept skipping from one thing to another because I couldn't seem to make myself get totally involved in any one thing.

In the middle of a book, I'd decide I just had to go shopping and buy myself some new jeans. And then once I was at Goldman's in town, the jeans looked boring and dull, and I bought myself a filmy blouse printed with zebras instead.

If I were happily playing with Peabody, I would suddenly get very guilty about having neglected the garden, and leave the startled Peabody in the middle of a swat-the-yarn game to rush outside with trowel and watering can and begin a feverish hour of hard work.

The trouble is, I told myself rather sternly one morning, and you'd better face it, you can't settle into doing anything because you keep waiting for the phone to ring.

I was standing in the den, having decided to dust, and I stopped with the grubby cloth in my hand and made a face at myself. Why had I let that thought out into the open to leer at me? I sighed, sitting down dejectedly. Well now that it was here I'd have to fool around and find some place for it, I supposed.

I hadn't really wanted David to call *immediately*, I acknowledged to myself. It had been nice just to go along dreamily remembering all of Sunday, reliving it, and letting all the warmth and love I'd felt for David swim over me.

I didn't want the phone to ring in the beginning and break in on that.

But it was Thursday now, and for the past two days I had been ducking feelings of depression. Was I wrong about David? Surely he had felt the same way I had. That kind of intensity couldn't be a one-way thing, could it? Didn't he, by now, just want to hear my voice again too?

I stirred uncomfortably. I'll call him up then, I decided. This is the last half of the twentieth century and my consciousness had been raised, hadn't it? I didn't need to play an old-fashioned coquette and wait for David.

But I stopped midway to the phone. What was I thinking of? I couldn't possibly call him. He'd be in the middle of his office hours; but it wasn't that. If I called him I would just stutter and stammer and act like a jackass, I'd be so nervous. I'd break and dissolve the bubble of Sunday forever, I thought, and promptly wondered whether indeed it *had* been just a bubble.

David? my mind called out to him. Don't do this, please don't.

I was jittery now, having worked myself up badly, and I knew I couldn't go back to doing anything as boring as dusting. I looked around me desperately, willing something to shoot out of the air and present itself as a solution to my quivering thoughts. And then my eye fell on the large orange pumpkin I'd bought yesterday and left sitting by the front door.

Carve the pumpkin! I told myself, and flew into the kitchen for a knife.

Creative, thought-absorbing, I muttered, scooping up the pumpkin and going outside with some hastily grabbed newspapers under my arm. It was a beautiful day, and it would be much less messy to do it out here.

I spread the newspapers out under a tree, sat in the sun, and began working.

In a few moments I had gotten involved, and the carving was something of a balm for me. At least my mind wasn't racing around sending out a lot of negative torture-thoughts.

"Tomorrow's Halloween," I told the face that was emerging under my hands. "You'll really have to look ugly."

I cut lots of jagged teeth and mean eyes, wondering why people always insisted on making smiling, friendly looking Jack O' Lanterns. After all, Halloween was supposed to scare the pants off you, wasn't it?

I realized I was carving with a bit more zeal than was necessary, but when I'd finished I was pleased with the results.

Tonight I'll pop corn and roast these seeds. That ought to kill a good hour, I thought with a nasty satisfaction as I placed my pumpkin on one of the front steps.

As I was gathering up the soaked, gluey newspapers from under the tree I saw Mrs. Harris and a child walking toward their house. The sight of them made me stop and stare hard.

Girl? Boy? It was impossible to tell. The child was dressed in overalls and was fair-haired. But that was all I could see. Anyhow, at that moment I was not occupied by thoughts of whether it was or wasn't a little girl. What I was looking at was much more important than that. I shook my head and squinted my eyes as a test. Yes, I thought, I'm almost sure . . . the child who was holding Mrs. Harris' hand was bigger than the one I'd seen sitting on the lawn with her.

I had to know for certain, and without wondering about my motives I lept into action, calling out "Mrs. Harris!" and sprinting across the grass and bushes that separated our houses.

The woman was at her door as my voice reached her, and she turned around with a start. "Wait a moment!" I called out and waved, but she just lifted her arm in quick recognition and hurried her child into the house. I stopped where I was, panting, my eyes focused on the closed door some fifteen yards ahead of me.

That rude, awful — my mind ran with epithets for Mrs. Harris, as I stood there trying to catch my breath. I wondered for a moment if I should go on up to the house anyway and knock, make her see me. But I couldn't do that. What reason could I give her? Outside, I might have made up something about Kate, but if I tracked her all the way into the house, that wouldn't be a reasonable excuse. I giggled, feeling a little giddy thinking about blowing her house down to tell her what a little charmer Kate was. Sense, Tanya dear, use your noodle.

Reluctantly I turned away, surprised, now that I was thinking more clearly, to discover how anxious I'd been to find out the truth about Kate's sibling for myself. Of course it wasn't just the little boy-girl thing that was troubling me. What had really spurred me into action was a growing belief that I had actually seen two *different* children with Mrs. Harris. But, I told myself, what if that were true? Unbelievable as it might seem to me, the Harrises *could* be having guests.

Well, the battle's over and I lost, I thought with a shrug. Let Mr. and Mrs. Paul Harris have a houseful of screaming brats. It had nothing to do with me.

I was probably using any distraction I could find to get my mind off David. Even thinking his name now was bringing lead to my steps and making me despair over ever having picked up the *Gloucester Daily Times* that lonely night in the library.

CHAPTER
NINE

On Halloween I sat around with my roasted pumpkin seeds and freshly popped corn and felt foolish. No one came.

I looked over at the tray I'd covered with an orange cloth and heaped with bowls of corn and nuts and reached to get a handful of the buttery popcorn for myself. Spinster with cat spends Halloween alone, I thought mournfully, chewing loudly in the empty house where I could hear my own watch ticking. And then, quite suddenly, I gave myself a good mental shake. I couldn't spend all of my time moaning around, dropping tears and sighs for David half the time and being fearful of the Harrises the other half.

I'd make myself go to that feminist group thing, I'd take a sketching class, I'd fill the days with *things* and not rot along in my own depression.

Just the thought of picking myself up and doing something made me restless and I got up quickly, deciding to wash the breakfast and lunch dishes. About time, I thought, running hot water in the sink and grimly rebuking myself for being such a slob.

It was late afternoon and the last rays of sun were slanting into the kitchen in dusty lines. A nice time of day, I mused, smelling the cool-air smells of earth and leaves. I looked out the window, a dish in my hand, picturing the lawns and trees ahead of me covered with snow. It was a pleasing scene, and I was just thinking about possibly getting my creaky ankles to stand up on ice skates that winter when I saw David.

Involuntarily I jumped back, thinking for a moment about hiding. But that would be ridiculous! David couldn't see me, he wasn't even looking in my direction. With a chilly shock of surprise I watched him get into his car, which was parked on the Harris' driveway. Even if I couldn't be sure it was David, which I could, I was certain of the car. His beat-up old blue Renault would have stood out wherever I saw it. I had, after all, been watching and waiting for it to pull up *my* driveway for the past week.

What was David doing coming out of the Harris'? And what possible reason could he have had for not telling me he knew them? Why, he must have known right along that it was his friend Mr. Harris who had injured Peabody! Why hadn't he said anything to me? I'd even told him how nervous those people had made me, and he'd just listened to it all and not offered a thing! Well, I had to amend, that wasn't strictly true of course. I hadn't wanted to get into the Harrises very deeply, and I *had* asked him to please stop talking about them. But still! He might have said something, anything!

I banged around in the kitchen, my irritation rising to wrath. What kind of dope did he think I was anyhow, I fumed, gladly letting my anger replace my pain. Anger, at least, was something I could deal with, expend myself on.

I had the vacuum cleaner plugged in and was violently running it around the living-room rug before I realized that I was copying my unloved aunt's favorite exercise for frustration — a lot of hard physical work. The realization made me snap the vacuum off and sink down onto the couch, exhausted without having any reason to be.

I sat still, thinking for a few moments, and then got up to put the cleaner away, feeling slightly better and calmer now that I'd made up my mind to do something. Tomorrow I would take Peabody to see Dr. Montserrat. To check on his leg, see if the cast could come off, whatever. It was a good excuse to see him and maybe find out exactly what was going on.

I started out with determination the next morning, putting Peabody in a small straw carrying case so that he wouldn't reinjure his leg in the car.

The tail end of my anger, mingled with my growing confusion, got me to David's without any qualms. But my confidence began to ebb rather quickly as I sat down in his waiting room next to a woman with two Scotties straining at their leashes. There were four people ahead of me, which for some reason I had not counted on, and so I had to prepare myself to wait — as calmly as I could.

In a few moments David came out to call his next patient, and then he saw me. He smiled broadly. I had the instant impression that he was glad to see me.

"Tanya!" he said, "everything all right?"

"Sure. Just a check-up."

"Won't be too long," he assured me and

disappeared with a woman dragging her recalcitrant German shepherd into his examining room.

My fingers and toes had gone quite cold and my heart was pumping irregularly by the time my turn came around. Several people had come in after me, and so I knew that I would not be able to take much of David's time.

"Well, how's Peabody then?" he asked, and I wondered if I had misread his smile before. Maybe he wasn't so very glad to see me at all. Maybe I had just received the professional smile he gave everyone.

"You didn't say, but I thought it was time you saw him again," I managed without a tremor. "Can his cast come off yet?"

David was busy examining and paid me little attention.

"He seems to be coming along just fine," he said at last, "but I think we'd better leave that cast on for a while yet."

"Oh." What did I say next? David was just looking at me, not offering anything. He seemed to be preoccupied, possibly even expecting and hoping I would scoop Peabody up and leave.

"I had a lovely time on Sunday," I burst out, rushing in before I could make any decision not to, and immediately hating myself for having given him even this much.

"I'm glad. I did too," he reacted with no expression for me to hold on to. And that was all. He obviously didn't have another word for me.

"Well," I gave him a difficult half-smile, "what do I owe you?"

"Not a thing," he replied pleasantly enough, and I decided not to protest. It seemed much too ridiculous.

"Thank you, David," was all I could think to say, and then I did pick up Peabody and leave.

Outside I drew a deep breath. "So, Peabody," I whispered to him softly, quelling the tears that had rushed into my eyes, "I guess that's that. I goofed. The man isn't interested."

But I was wrong. The minute my phone rang that evening, I knew I was wrong. It couldn't possibly be a wrong number, or somebody peddling insurance. It had to be David, and it was.

"Tanya?"

"Hello, David." There was certainly no sense in pretending I didn't know who it was.

"How are you?" Was this the way the conversation was really going to go? I *had* seen him that morning.

"I'm all right," I replied, struggling to get a hint of coolness into my voice, while being careful not to keep up this social-amenities conversation by asking, "And how are you?"

"Your voice sounds strange. Is there anything the matter?"

"No, not a thing." I admitted to a real pleasure that he'd called, but I didn't intend to make anything easy for him.

"Not having any more trouble with your neighbors, are you?"

I couldn't believe he was really asking me that! Well, anyhow, he wasn't going to get a truthful answer.

"No, I'm not."

"Tanya?"

"Yes."

"You're angry with me, aren't you?"

"Oh, David, I thought you'd call. And then when I saw you today you were so . . . so . . ." I faltered, hung somewhere between release, and fury at myself for having spoken out.

"Unresponsive," he finished for me, and I thought I could hear the familiar smile in his voice.

But I couldn't find any words to answer him yes.

"I'm sorry, Tanya. I know I was. I'd had a really difficult morning, and then seeing you kind of threw me, I suppose."

Had he had a difficult morning or a difficult evening the night before? I wondered

111

suddenly. And why had seeing me been such a big surprise? Or maybe the truth was that he'd just overextended himself on Sunday.

"Hey," David said gently into the phone, and the tone of his voice made me feel wobbly.

"Hey yourself," I said, hearing forgiveness all over my voice.

"What are we going to do together Saturday night?" he wanted to know.

"I have no idea," I told him. "What?"

"I'll think of something," David assured me. "Six o'clock all right for you?"

It was fine for me. Beautiful! And I said so, curbing as much enthusiasm as I could.

I hung up feeling better than I had in days. I even felt capable of eating a proper meal. Then, just as I was thinking up a delicious concoction for myself, the lights went out.

I gave a startled gasp and knew a moment of pure terror before I shook myself off and realized that it probably had something to do with fuses.

I fumbled my way into the den to find Raymond's instructions, but when I'd finally located the fuse box upstairs I couldn't see that anything had blown.

Now what do I do? I wondered. Maybe it's not a fuse, I thought, and felt my way to an upstairs window. But the lights were on in the Harris house, so presumably it did have something to do with that box.

I fiddled around for a while, replacing fuses haphazardly, but nothing happened. And I most definitely did not like the idea of spending the entire evening without electricity. I knew it would make me jumpy. Take way Johnny Carson or the late movie these nights and I'd run my fingernails down to my knuckles.

I was being foolish, I decided finally. I would just have to go over to the Harris' and ask for help. On my way out the door, I momentarily played with the idea of calling David back and appealing to him. But I gave that up as being entirely too helplessly feminine. And this was certainly no time to take advantage of David, when things were perhaps much more sketchy between us than I wanted to believe.

The lawns and trees were lightened by a full moon, and after the absolute darkness inside it was a relief to be in a more natural world. Just nighttime outdoors, with stars filling the evening sky and the sounds of late-fall crickets adding to the peaceful, slumbering night.

No need then for my heart to be jerking against my ribs and for a thin film of moisture to begin spreading over my body. The Harris house was only a few steps away now, and my mind was telling me how much I didn't want to approach it.

Oh, pull yourself together, you dumb goose, I rebuked, and made myself march firmly up to the front door and stab at the bell. I waited, taking a deep breath, hearing nothing. I rang again — there'd been lights, someone must be home. But still no sound came from inside, and I had the peculiar and very unpleasant feeling that I was being observed. Someone inside was looking at me and waiting me out. I felt crawly.

But then I shook myself and clenched my wet hands into balls determinedly. I'd go around to the side of the house where the other door was and try there.

The lights I'd seen were on the side of the house, but all the shades and been pulled tightly down and I couldn't see inside. This door had no bell and so I knocked sharply on the peeling wood, beginning to feel rather desperate.

Then, at last, I did hear a noise from inside, and in a moment I caught the sound of feet approaching the door.

"Who is it?" The voice was thin and female, and I breathed relief. Maybe the monster-husband was not home.

"It's Tanya Sohier. From next door," I added.

"Yes?" The voice floated out to me, but the door remained firmly closed. I had been right about this woman — she was terribly rude. Either that, or she was just plain stupid. Was she really going to let me stand out here, calling my problem in to her?

"I wonder . . . could you open the door? I need your help." There, that ought to do it, I thought. For a moment nothing happened, and then a lock rasped and the door opened.

Mrs. Harris stood in the dim light of a hallway, dressed in a faded wrapper, her frizzy hair skinned back.

"I rang the front doorbell, but no one . . ."

"Don't work," she replied, but made no movement to step back and let me enter.

"Oh." I shivered suddenly in the cool night air. "May I come in?" I asked her, surprising myself by the question. I could just have explained my problem at the door. But some perversity, mixed, I'm sure, with curiosity, made me attempt to find a way into this house.

She opened the door wider and I stepped inside.

"Better come along to the kitchen," she said to me grudgingly and I followed her along a damp-smelling hall and into an untidy kitchen with worn linoleum on the floor and crusty dishes sitting on the table and drain.

115

I wrinkled my nose at an unpleasant, stale, eggy smell and thought what an unhappy atmosphere this must be for Kate.

"What can I do for you, Miz?"

Startled out of my reverie I blinked at Mrs. Harris, who looked even more distressing in the neon glare of the kitchen.

She hadn't asked me to sit down, but, stubbornly, I sat anyhow. I was pretty sure Paul wasn't around and I was not going to let myself be treated badly by her.

"I called to you outside the other day when you were with your little girl, but you didn't answer me," I found myself saying, as amazed at my own words as the shocked look on her face told me she was.

But, "Ya did?" was her noncommittal reply. Clearly she was not treating this as a social call and was waiting impatiently for me to tell her why I was here.

"Yes. You do have a little girl don't you?" And at her nod, I went on audaciously, "I really was mistaken then. When I first spoke to Kate I was sure she told me she had a baby *brother*." There, I thought, satisfied with myself, let her chew on that one for a while.

"Nope. Got another little girl." Her reply was toneless, but she added incomprehensively, "Kids don't pay much attention."

"What's her name?" I shot out, not quite understanding my motives.

"She's called Bethie, Miss, and right now she's not too well, so if you'll tell me what you come about, I kin get back to her."

Well, I supposed that was explaining the situation to me all right! I subsided a bit, feeling slightly ashamed of myself. I had no right to come in here and fire questions at this woman. It was just that once inside, and face to face with her again, I couldn't seem to help myself. I guess I just badly wanted her to clear things up for me, so that I would feel more at ease, having the Harrises as my neighbors.

"I'm sorry," I murmured, "about your Bethie, I mean. Is there anything I can do to help?"

Mrs. Harris shook her head and I could see a faint hostility creep into her eyes. Oooops, I thought, I'd better just ask her about the fuse box and get out of here.

"All my lights went out," I explained quickly. "I tried putting new fuses in, but nothing worked. I wondered if you'd have any idea — "

"Got a circuit breaker over to your place?" she asked me, and as she said those words tiny little bells pinged in my head and my thoughts flipped back to something Raymond had said. What was it? "Of course there's a circuit breaker. If any or all the lights blow you just throw that. . . ." I even remembered him saying something

117

about it being too obvious to bother writing down for me.

I nodded embarrassedly at Mrs. Harris. "I do. I forgot about it."

"Well, then you're all set," Mrs. Harris said to me in a voice that pushed me to the door. "Ye just throw that there switch and yer lights'll come on."

"Right," I said, although I made no immediate move to leave. I was trying desperately to think of something to say that would detain me.

Just as the silence between us was becoming almost ominous, I heard sounds coming from the upstairs of the house. Terrible mewling sounds at first, and then a frail voice that cried, "Mama, Mama."

For a moment neither of us moved. I was frozen by those cries. That word repeated over and over sounded so pathetic, so lost. I shivered and tears filled my eyes.

Slowly, I was aware of another voice, Mrs. Harris', and her face looming and leering in front of mine. "I've got to go up to her. I tole ya she wuz sick!"

"I'll go with you. I'll help," I told her quickly.

"You'll go *home*!" she fairly shouted at me. "I don't want no one up there with her exceptin' me, hear? You got what you wanted and you leave right now."

She had her hand on my arm and I allowed her to steer me to the door. I did not, after all, belong here. These people didn't want my help, or, I realized grimly, even my presence.

"I hope . . . I hope Bethie will be all right," I told Mrs. Harris, but she only made an unpleasant grunt, her mouth tight, and shut the door in my face.

Although I was relieved to be outside, away from those sounds that had caught at me and seemed to squeeze something into a hard, tight lump in my stomach, bringing back all those years after my parents were killed, I felt suddenly that I should not have left. I should have stayed, gone up to Bethie, helped her.

But what was I thinking! Her mother was there; a stranger would only confuse and frighten her. Yet as I made my way back to the Rinns', I couldn't shake off a feeling of dread. An awful forboding crept into me and turned my body icy-cold.

CHAPTER TEN

I spent a restless night, filled with nightmares that kept waking me up shuddering and shivering, trying to convince myself that if I allowed sleep to come again, the dreams wouldn't recur. But of course they did.

The next morning I woke up feeling spent and exhausted. I also looked it, I realized, recoiling from the bathroom mirror in distaste. There were dark smudges under my eyes and my skin was pale and shiny looking.

I drank almost a full quart of orange juice, hoping it would have some restorative effect. Of course it didn't. I kept finding myself being drawn to windows in the house that faced the Harris'. I don't know what I expected to see or hear, but nothing at all was happening over there. Just a plain dark house, standing in a field with trees around it.

I would find out about Bethie, I finally resolved. Somehow I would crash through those ugly, awful-people and learn for myself that she was fine.

This thought had been gathering in me since last night, and I realized now that it was slowly becoming obsessive. At the moment I was filled with the frustration of knowing that there was nothing, just now, that I *could* do. But somehow I would find a way, I assured myself firmly. I did not bother to question why it was so important that I should.

As I dressed to go out with David, it struck me that maybe he would provide a way for me. At least a clue to let me know more than I did now. But I would have to be careful with what I said to David, and how I said it, I realized with a start, suddenly remembering that he had not voluntecred anything to me about his relationship with the Harrises. But I had not really seen or talked to him much since I'd watched him leaving their house on Halloween, so possibly he just hadn't had a chance to explain.

Well, I decided, tugging a brush through

my snarled hair, tonight he'd have his chance.

I was startled to realize how completely any thoughts of David had been swept from my mind. Bethie Harris had totally absorbed me, and it did not even seem peculiar that this was so. But now, waiting for David to come, all the deep, good feelings I'd had for him came washing back. I was once again enfolded in the warmth and security I'd felt when we'd been together. Dear David. He would help me make all of this come out right.

The door knocker sounded and I leaped up. It's David, dope, I told myself the next moment, furious that I was reacting so sharply to things lately. Why should a simple thing like a knock on the door make me almost senseless with fear?

This time David's smile was wide and deep, his pleasure at seeing me so obvious that I immediately forgot all my fears that maybe he didn't feel the same as I did.

"May I come in for a moment, or would that be scandalous?" he asked with the familiar laugh in his voice as I hedged at the door.

I pretended to look around furtively. "Quick! Before anyone sees you," I told him, and he slipped by me, heading into the living room.

"I've missed you."

"Me, too," I said, smiles galloping all over my face. And then I noticed a tissue-wrapped package he'd put down on the table.

"What's that?"

"For you," David indicated with a nod. "Go ahead, open it."

I felt a childish excitement as I reached for the package. I hadn't received a gift from anyone I cared about since my parents died, and a well-remembered Christmas-morning feeling swept over me as I began to tear away at the paper and ribbon. My hands touched something soft and fuzzy and I drew a small brown gorilla out of the wrappings.

"Oh, David!" I breathed happily, pressing the little animal with the tiny pink tongue and miniscule yellow head-bow to me. "How wonderful!"

"Her name's Georgiana."

"It is? How do you know?" I asked him, rubbing a finger along the smooth velvet face and touching the two little button eyes. I was lost in happiness. When was the last time anyone had given me something like this? My thoughts traced back to a birthday when I was ten and my father had come home, struggling up our front steps, carrying a panda that was bigger than I was. But this time the thought of my parents did not bring tears. I was able to remember happily and feel a tenderness grow inside me.

"Did you hear me?" David's voice broke through my thoughts.

"No." I cradled Georgiana to me. "What?"

"You asked me how I knew what her name was."

"Right. I did. And what did you say?"

"I said she had a tag on her that said so."

"Oh, David, you're so imaginative!" I laughed. And then I was walking over to David and putting my arms around his neck and kissing him. Again I wondered where this new person inside me was coming from. But at the moment I liked her too much to really care.

Somehow I made myself get disentangled from David. "I thought you were taking me out for dinner," I accused him, and he snapped his fingers. "Right!" I'd forgotten all about it."

"Shall we take Georgiana along with us?" I suggested.

David groaned, and then he looked at me closely. "Are you serious?"

"Well, maybe just a little," I replied, knowing that I would find no embarrassment in having Georgiana as a third at our table. But I was easily able to allow for David's having different sensibilities.

"Never mind," I told him. "I'll just put her somewhere out of Peabody's reach."

We drove into Boston for dinner. It was a restaurant that David was so eager to try that I couldn't bring myself to tell him I'd just as soon eat in Gloucester.

It was a nice place, not fancy, but richly old, and with a huge menu with extravagant prices.

"Mmmmm," I mumbled, studying the right-hand side of the menu.

"Decide what you want to eat, Tanya," David admonished me, "and stop worrying about the prices."

"Do vets really make this kind of money?"

"Well, this one makes enough to be able to afford these prices about once every six months."

"I think I'm very glad that I came along during one of those six-month periods," I told him in a voice as light as I could make it.

"So am I," David said, with a look so serious on his face that I buried myself behind the oversized menu and tried not to think about all the things I was feeling.

David ordered lavishly — all kinds of good things, including stuffed artichokes and a bottle of sparkling Burgundy. Afterwards, we lolled back in the armchairs that were our seats and contemplated each other silently and happily.

"Lovely," I murmured, "just lovely," and David nodded.

Then, seemingly from out of nowhere, a snapshot of the Harrises appeared in my mind. I roused myself, struggling to sit up straight and gain a little composure.

My heart had begun to thud uncomfortably and I wondered whether it was the wine or the realization that I was going to have to talk to David about that odious couple and bring something unpleasant into this perfect evening.

"David," I began, and he reached over and took my hand, making things doubly hard for me. Now where to begin? I wondered helplessly. "David," I repeated.

"You remembered my name!" he replied jokingly, as I tried to give him my best shaky smile.

"I have to talk to you."

"All right." He looked at me. "Why so serious, Tanya?"

But that was a question I couldn't answer. When I made myself ask him what I had to, he would understand. I hoped. I could feel my body stiffen and I withdrew my hand from David's. If I could manage to keep my voice straight, he didn't need to know how nervous I was.

"You know the Harrises, don't you?" I

blurted out, having found no easier or better way to say it. After I'd said the words, I felt a sense of release. Not very diplomatically put, but at least I'd finally asked.

"Why, yes. I do." Was I imagining it, or was David really visibly withdrawing from me?

I waited, but it didn't seem as if he were going to add anything to this. Oh, damn, I agonized, this whole thing really was going to be a mess.

"I wondered," I fumbled, looking for words, "why you hadn't said." I paused, but still nothing was coming from David so I trudged on, "I . . . I mean when I told you about Peabody you . . . you never mentioned anything . . . and then later. I just thought — "

"How did you know I knew them?" David cut in, lacerating my hesitation with a clear, unencumbered question. I both envy and dislike people who can remain cool and logical in the midst of almost anything. In David's case, I pushed off the dislike part, dwelling on envying him his calm, unruffled attitude.

"I saw you. On Halloween night. I saw you leaving their house."

But David seemed to have no remark to make to this either. I badly wanted to shake him, to force some reaction from him. I suddenly felt as if I were sharing my evening with a stranger, and the feeling made me very distressed. It was amazing to me how David could seem so beautifully close sometimes and then become so distant.

"Aren't you going to say *anything*?" I demanded suddenly, unable to bear the strangeness that was building between us.

"Arlene Harris is my cousin." Again the terse answer with no emotional response from David.

But the words. They snagged in my head. David related to that? Now the whole thing really did seem impossible.

"Why didn't you tell me?" I asked him as calmly as I could. I felt myself entering the first throes of anger, and I did not want to begin a scene with David in this terribly proper, austere, and expensive restaurant.

David sighed, rubbing the bridge of his nose as if he were weary, or as if I were boring him awfully. "When I first met you and heard about Peabody, Tanya, I didn't know who your neighbors were. Later, it didn't seem significant." He spoke stiffly, which might have been a warning to me, but by that time I was beyond caring. David was treating me like a dreary acquaintance, and I knew that I meant a lot more than that to him, didn't I?

"What do you mean 'significant,' " I exploded. "What would it have taken to make it significant? Those people, I'm sorry to have to say this to you, David, if you're related to her, but those people — " I broke off, not being sure of my words.

"Yes? What about them, Tanya?"

"There's something wrong there — with the two of them, I mean. Not Kate. She's fine and solid. I like her, David. But Paul and Arlene — is that what you said her name was? — they're both .. well, you just don't — "

"You're right, Tanya, I don't," he said, interrupting me again; but since I was floundering, I didn't much mind. David continued in a voice that was softer now, and more gentle. Tones that made me begin to relax a little. "The thing is, I don't want to know. At least if I don't have to. So long as they're not bothering you or Peabody anymore, I don't want to hear about them. I didn't know Arlene and her family were going to move up here. Hearing from her was a terrific surprise for me. We've never been close, and I have no need to cultivate a relationship with them now. But as far as anything being wrong with them, I don't know what you mean. Paul is not the greatest mind I've come across, but then neither was Arlene, so," he said with a dry laugh, "it seems they ought to have a fairly equal, if not good marriage."

I didn't know where to go after David said all that. Telling him my fears now began to seem foolish. He would probably think I was exaggerating, and besides, as he had just told me, he wasn't really interested, so long as I was all right. And I was all right, wasn't I? Besides I had ruined enough of this evening already, I thought unhappily.

"Did you meet Kate?" I asked in a voice which strived to give in a little, but not entirely abandon the conversation. I thought, if possible, David and I had a little further to go with this. But I would try to continue carefully. I didn't want to see that coldness slipping over him again.

David frowned. "Briefly," he said.

"Didn't you like her, Daivd?" I went on eagerly, somehow needing to talk about Kate first, possibly wanting him to reassure me that his cousin and her husband would be good to her, take the right kind of care of her. Also it was a lead-in for me to talk about Bethie.

"I didn't think much about her one way or the other," David shrugged, and for an awful moment I thought maybe he just didn't like children.

But then he grinned at me. "I gather you would like to swoop down and rescue Kate from those undesirable parents of hers."

"It wouldn't be a bad idea," I muttered. "Kate and Bethie too."

"Bethie? Oh, you mean the little girl?"

"Yes, David. I think there's something really wrong there, with Bethie," I went on eagerly. "She's very sick or something, I think, and — "

David was holding up a hand, as if to ward me off. "Okay, Tanya, no more now," he warned in a voice that asked for no arguments. "I told you, I really don't want to get involved in talking about them anymore." He looked away from me for a moment, toward the dimly lighted table next to ours. "It's just too bad that you have to be living next door to them," he said, almost as if he were talking to himself.

"Yes, well," I fumbled, "I guess I'd better just leave it alone now." I looked down into my lap, feeling much like a child who has just been chastised.

Then I felt David's fingers lifting my chin. His voice spoke to me softly, caressingly, "Come on, dear, don't look so serious and unhappy. We've been having a nice evening, haven't we?"

"Yes."

"Then let's continue having one."

And of course we did. We walked along the narrow streets of Boston, David pointing out everything historic that we passed and me loving every moment of it. But beneath my enjoyment and chatter, I was feeling both unsure and a little nervous.

I loved David. I knew that, but there were parts of him I didn't understand, and they made me uncomfortable, unsure of myself with him. The way he could slip into a dark mood without my being able to follow or understand why it had happened. All the odd parts of David seemed to be tied up with the Harrises, but my knowing this was no comfort. What was so wrong that he wouldn't talk about them, and had virtually forbidden me to mention them?

CHAPTER
ELEVEN

On Monday morning a long, rambling letter came from Anne, and reading it made me feel oddly homesick. I needed someone like Anne in my life now. Someone I could talk to, confide my fears in. For a while I toyed with the idea of writing her a manifesto, telling Anne, finally, all that had been going on since she and Raymond left. It would be such a relief to let it all out with the realization that it would be reaching a compassionate, understanding ear.

I even went as far as dragging out their typewriter and writing several paragraphs which, as soon as I'd read them over, made me realize that I could never send Anne this kind of letter. Everything I'd written sounded so awful and macabre that either she would have wanted to come flying home to help, or else I would succeed in totally wrecking the rest of her trip, which had almost another eleven months to go. I shuddered. Eleven more months of the Harrises. But then there would be eleven more months of David too. . . .

I tore the paper out of the typewriter and ripped it into small pieces, as if I were afraid someone would come snooping and discover all my hidden thoughts.

I slid another paper into the typewriter and tried again. I'd been neglecting writing to Anne because it was so difficult to write a friendly, warm letter without really *saying* anything. Of course, I suddenly decided, I could write her just about David, my feelings for him. That would be real, and Anne would certainly care.

I sighed with relief and began pecking away again. It took me two hours to write the letter, and when I reread it, I found that I was totally satisfied. All the good things I had with David had come through, and it was lovely to be able to say them sort of out loud at last.

I was so pleased that I decided to drive down to the post office and mail it right away. I think I was also a little afraid that I would have second thoughts about having exposed so much of me to someone else. I've always been pretty private, but now was a time for me to be open, and to give part of me to Anne, whom I realized with a small shock that I loved.

Anne and David in such a short time. It was lovely to have found two people to care about in such different and yet such deep ways.

And you almost didn't want to come up here, I rebuked myself, humming along the harbor road and delighting in the cold, white sunshine.

David had called me Sunday afternoon, and we'd had a long, leisurely conversation, me with my legs tucked up on the couch and sipping endless cups of coffee from a pot I'd brought into the den with me. It was a lovely, relaxing hour we spent together over the phone. And when I hung up I felt better about David. No little weird things had crept into our conversation. I began to be soothed and to forget that there were any snags at all in our relationship.

A few days later I was out on the driveway, having decided to give Raymond's car a badly needed waxing. I had the car radio on and was very involved with rubbing away and singing lustily along with John Denver, which is probably why I didn't notice the arrival of Paul Harris.

"Get yer lights workin' all right?" he said in a loud, rough voice that made me whirl around in surprise.

"Oh! Yes, thank you, I did," I said, keeping my voice slightly cool and turning back to my waxing.

"The wife told me you wuz over. Sorry I wuzn't home." I wasn't looking, but I could hear the leer in his voice. What was he doing over here anyhow? Maybe if I paid absolutely no attentiton to him, he'd leave, I thought, but realized it wasn't a very realistic idea.

He came around to the front of the car so that we could watch each other's faces, and unfortunately I was too awkward to turn and begin on the rear bumper. Too obvious. I didn't want him to see how much his presence upset me. I'd just wait him out. After all, we were outside. What could possibly happen to me here that I couldn't handle?

But it seemed that Mr. Harris wasn't going to talk. He was just going to lean on the fender of the car and watch me. After a few moments of this I began to feel very uneasy, which served to open my mouth and make me begin yammering about the first thing I could think of.

"I see you've got your house all fixed up for winter," I jabbered at him.

"What?" he scowled.

"The boards. Kate said — "

"Oh yeah? What did she say?" Once again Paul Harris was turning nasty. I took a second to think how easy it was for me to produce this reaction in him.

"She just said that you'd put up the boards against the bad weather," I answered, annoyed at the slight tremble I detected in my voice.

"Yeah, winter, that's right," he mumbled to me. "Anything else you'd like to know, Miss Nosy Parker?"

"What do you mean?" I asked, stopping any pretense at work and facing him directly. "You have no right to talk to me like that!" I felt a little better now that he had made me angry.

"No right, no right," he mimicked, making me wonder if he'd been drinking again.

"How . . . how is your baby?" I tried, wondering at the same time why I was bothering. But maybe, if I could get him to react kind of normally for a change, I might feel better.

"My baby? How's my baby, you want to know?"

"Yes," I swallowed, "Bethie. Your wife told me she was sick."

"Damn kid squeaks and squalls alla time," he glowered. "No peace with that one around."

Oh you ugly, horrible, miserable man, I thought.

"I . . . excuse me," I said, gathering up the wax and my rag. "I've got to go in now."

"You do? How come?" He stood directly in front of me, almost as if he were barring my way.

Another bump of fear. "I have things to do if you don't mind."

"But you wuz already doin' things out here. Seems to me, Miss, you been doin' all kindsa things since you got here."

"I'm sorry, Mr. Harris, but I don't understand what you're talking about. Now if you'll just excuse — "

"I ain't finished yet. I mean ta tell you ta keep to yer own self if ya don' mind."

"Keep to myself? How? What are you talking about?" I demanded, not knowing now whether I was more angry or frightened.

"You're a smart girl. You figure it out," he said elliptically. And then as I was just standing there spluttering over what to say, he turned and left me, heading across the lawn with a slightly weaving motion.

I stood and watched him go, feeling both relieved and shaken. I seemed to be suffering quite a lot lately from a mixture of those two emotions, I reflected wryly, continuing on into the house. All pleasure of being outside and working on the car was gone for me then.

I spent that evening as I had spent others — reflecting about the Harrises. This night, however, I came up with a quite new thought. One that made me more repulsed and frightened than I'd been before.

It happened quite by chance. After dinner, weary from Harris-thought, I wandered into the living room and picked up an old issue of *Psychology Today* that the Rinns had left, among others, in the magazine rack.

I leafed idly through the magazine and then stopped on a page about halfway through. My fingers clutched the paper after I had read the name of the article, and for a while the text of it was just a blur in front of my eyes.

I breathed deeply, and then made myself read the article through slowly and carefully. It dealt with cruelty to children, parental cruelty, and by the time I had finshed reading the last horrifying word, I was sure I had a good part of the answer to the problem next door.

Inexplicably, my eyes filled with tears which began pouring down my cheeks — in a few moments I was sobbing. Maybe for all the lost, lonely years of my own childhood, and then in anger and frustration for what I was now convinced was the cause of those awful cries I had heard at the Harris'. I thought about the cruelty so evident in Paul Harris and the wooden, stunned look of the child I'd seen on the lawn. This child, I had begun to convince myself, must indeed be the same one I'd seen with Arlene Harris and whom I'd heard crying. It had probably been a trick of light, something that had made me think they were two separate children.

I shuddered and tried to make myself stop crying. I badly needed someone, David, here to comfort me. But just now I didn't have the strength to go to the phone, call him, and pour out all my ugly suspicions. Besides, a small voice went off inside me: David doesn't want to hear.

Finally I got myself in hand and went into the downstairs bathroom to douse my face with cold water. That revived me some, and I went slowly back into the living room, walking painfully, as if I were recovering from a debilitating illness.

I stretched out on the couch and tried to think clearly. In a few moments Peabody found me and pounced up onto my stomach. My arms went around him automatically and I squeezed him to me until he began to meow in protest.

"What if you had still been living there, Peabody? What would they have done to you?" As I spoke aloud to the kitten, my thoughts turned to Kate, and here I paused, indecisive for the first time about my conclusions. The article had *seemed* to be the answer. More, I *felt* that it must be so, but I hadn't thought of Kate. She was all right, wasn't she? No one had been beating her; there were no scars there. I let myself go back and remember every time I'd spoken to Kate, particularly the times either of her parents had been mentioned. What had her reactions to them been? I shut my eyes tight and tried to remember. But I could come up with nothing alarming. Kate had seemed, at different times, a little wary of her parents, of disobeying or displeasing them. But that was all. I had detected no real fear in her, I was certain of that. If I had, I would have been aware of it at the time. And I would certainly remember it now, when I was trying so hard in my mind to indict the Harrises.

My thoughts cooled and slowed and I suddenly felt very tired. I must have just gone off half-crazy when I read that article, I thought drowsily. If they were hurting Kate's sister, she would know about it, surely. She would try to stop them, or certainly show some signs herself of being deeply disturbed, wouldn't she?

My eyes were burning and heavy and I allowed my lids to droop down over them.

Sleep would be such a relief, and I was so terribly tired...

But, unfortunately, exhausted as I was, sleep would not come. In a little while all that lovely, relaxed sleepiness had left me, and I was sitting up again, my heart beating fast, holding Peabody on my lap and staring straight ahead, remembering my bout with Paul Harris that afternoon. He had warned me — told me to keep to myself, stay away from them. The threat, if I did dare to interfere, had been obvious in his eyes.

True, I couldn't explain how Kate had remained unscathed, but I couldn't entirely put that article off to my flying imagination either. Somewhere the truth was slumbering, and I meant to find it out for myself.

CHAPTER TWELVE

The next afternoon, on my way back from a friendly gossip with Mrs. Collins (I had gone there to see if she had any more information about the Harrises to impart, but she'd only prodded me for anything *I* might know), I passed Kate on the road.

Pulling over to the side, I called out to her, "Hop in."

For once she didn't hesitate at all.

"Thank you, Tanya, I was getting cold. My mother *told* me I should have worn my heavier jacket to school." Kate flopped her books down on the seat next to me and seemed quite content.

Not exactly the victim of child-beating, I thought ruefully. And that stuff about

Arlene Harris worrying over what she wore to school ... well, it all didn't add up to a very nasty picture. I shook my head. Had I really been that far off last night?

Kate was chattering on to me — something about homework and the perfectly rotten teacher she had lucked into. I turned my mind off and tried to concentrate on what she was saying.

As we approached the Rinns', I slowed down. "Want to come in and have a snack with me?" I invited her, reflecting that I seemed to be forever bribing Kate's stomach.

She wriggled forward in her seat and squinted through the windshield. "My father isn't home," she replied candidly, "so I guess it will be all right."

I pulled into the driveway and stopped the car. "What has your father got to do with your coming in?" I asked, turning to her.

Kate giggled a little and then slapped a hand over her mouth. "Woops. I think maybe I shouldn't have said that."

"What do you mean, Kate? Doesn't your father want you visiting me?" I accused, at the same time wanting to spirit her away and into the house before Paul Harris' car should pull up.

"*Visiting* you? I don't even think he

wants me *talking* to you," Kate went on conspiratorially. She gathered up her books. "Come on, Tanya, let's go before he comes and I have to go straight home."

I got out of the car and let Kate in with some misgivings. If her father didn't want her here, I should probably not allow her to come in, I thought with a prick of conscience.

But of course I did, settling us in the den with Kate on the floor crooning to Peabody. "How does hot chocolate sound? It'll warm you up," I invited.

"Delicious," Kate said enthusiastically, and I headed for the kitchen to boil some milk.

I came back shortly, bearing huge mugs of hot chocolate with a generous amount of marshmallows bobbling around in them.

"This is super," Kate told me, drinking with relish.

In a few moments her mouth was coated with froth and I had an overwhelming desire to hug her to me and not allow her back into that house.

"You know my mother's cousin, David Montserrat, don't you?" she asked me, and I was startled by my own surprise at her question.

"Well, yes, I do," I answered, hesitating and for some reason feeling a little embarrassed. "How did you know?"

"Oh, I just heard them talking when David was there last night — "

"David was at your house last night?" I interrupted her to ask in astonishment.

"Oh, sure," Kate replied airily, "he's been before too."

"Yes, I know," I said faintly. My head whirled. What was happening? I wondered fearfully. Just what was going on? And what had been said about me? I badly wanted to know that, but could think of no way to ask Kate without her realizing I was pumping her for information.

"So," I began on a drawn breath, knowing I had to change the subject, "how come your father doesn't want you to visit me, or talk to me, even?" It was probably unfair to question Kate this way, yet she had volunteered the information and I needed an answer from her.

But now Kate's daring was gone. Possibly she was having second thoughts about being someplace she wasn't supposed to be?

She tried to shrug it off. "Oh, I don't know. He just gets these weird ideas sometimes."

However, I was not going to let her off this easily. "What do you mean? What weird ideas?"

Kate blushed painfully and I gave myself a good, hard, mental slap. It was ugly of me to take advantage and cause her such distress, but right now it seemed that Kate was the only one, including David, I thought, wincing, who might tell me the truth.

I reached out and took one of her cold hands in mine. "It's all right, Kate," I tried reassuring. She looked at me questioningly, not knowing what to say. "I mean I know your father isn't too fond of me," I went on, not quite knowing where I was going, but trying to say something that would give Kate back her dignity. I knew that by now she was very sorry she had said anything at all, and certainly she was regretting having come home with me.

Kate let her hand stay in mine, and I could see that it took an effort for her to speak. But she was going to try to explain, and I felt a good, solid warmth for her wash over me.

"I guess it's that my father's just not very friendly," she tried, frowning. Well, I thought with some irony, that was one way of putting it!

"I mean I don't think he even has just one friend in the whole world, and he thinks that you ... you ..."

"That I'm too nosy, doesn't he?" I helped out. And Kate nodded wordlessly, relieved that this was out and over with.

"I'm sorry he feels that way." I spoke more stiffly than I'd meant to and saw Kate beginning to freeze up on me again.

"He just doesn't know you, I guess, like I do, you know," she coaxed me in a low voice, and I quickly reached out for a way to tell her that her father didn't matter to me, that it was, after all, Kate herself who was important.

"Well, let's not us worry about it, Kate," I said, patting her hand and giving it a squeeze. "We're friends anyway. And whenever it's easy for you, you know I want to see you."

She smiled happily, and we both relaxed into cocoa drinking and playing with Peabody, who was delighting in showing off for Kate.

A loud knocking on the back door interrupted us. Kate looked up questioningly at me and I had to tell her, as gently as possible, "I think that might be someone about you."

"Oh wow, if it's my father, I'm in for it," she said, but look as hard as I could at her, I could detect no terror in her face, just the usual childhood fear of a possible punishment coming.

For myself, heading for the kitchen, I dearly hoped it was not Paul Harris' face I would be confronted with. And I was lucky — Arlene Harris greeted me at the door with her usual nervous twitch.

"Is Kate with you?" she spoke without a greeting.

"Yes, she is. Won't you come in, Mrs. Harris?" I set my teeth to be polite to her.

Without answering, or making a move, she peered around me and called into the house: "Kate! Come on. Come on home now."

And then Kate appeared in the kitchen, with her school books tucked under her arm and a sheepish expression on her face.

"I'm sorry, Mother. Tanya picked me up on the road, and I just wanted to stop in and see Peabody," she said in a cajoling voice.

"Yeah? Well, come along home now. Yer father'll be here any minute." Mrs. Harris was upset, but she didn't seem to be very angry with her daughter.

Kate turned to me. "Thank you, I enjoyed being here," she said in that old-fashioned, quite proper way she had.

"Me too," I replied, giving her shoulder a slight hug and catching the look of disapproval on Mrs. Harris' face.

Kate moved away from me quickly, but her eyes on mine were warm and happy.

After they left I wondered how much hugging and kissing Kate got at home. Then I gave it up, thinking that at least *she* certainly wasn't being beaten.

Two days and a wet, sleety snowfall passed, and again I hadn't heard from David.

"What kind of game is he playing?" I asked Georgiana who was cuddled up on my comforter and seemed to regard me with sympathetic eyes. "It's been over a week," I accused her, "and he's even been over to see that cousin of his whom he supposedly doesn't like!"

It was too ugly to be outdoors and I went about the house cleaning desultorily and fuming with real energy. "Is this supposed to be a picturesque New England snow?" I asked the view of bleak gray slushy lawn. "Yuck!" I made a face at the weather and finally settled down to read the *Gloucester Daily Times*.

That was when I saw the story about the kidnapping and began reversing my "cruelty to children" theory for what seemed to me a more possible one.

It had happened, of all places, in Peabody, and what I was reading was a follow-up story of a kidnapping that had taken place weeks ago. How had I missed it then? I wondered, reading on and doing rapid mental calculations about when I had first seen the Harris' daughter. I was a little confused about time, but it seemed to me that the little girl in Peabody had been taken from her yard at a date that would approximate when I had first seen Bethie. It did dovetail, I assured myself. A five-and-a-half-year-old child, fair-haired, named Terry. Well, the name didn't matter.

I read the story over again. Ransom had been asked for, but had not been picked up at the appointed place. The police had finally been called in, and now, it seemed, no one knew just what was happening.

Strangely, I was reacting very calmly to this. If I could keep my thoughts off Bethie for a bit, I could concentrate and see what would be best for me to do to find out if this time my suspicions would be confirmed. What I couldn't do, right off, was call the police. If I were wrong and, of course, I admitted to myself, thére was every reason to suppose I might be, I would never get Paul Harris off my back. If he found out I had called the police and the kidnapping had nothing at all to do with the Harrises, he'd make my life even more of a hell than it already was.

I played with the possibility of sending an anonymous note to the police, and then I realized that that wouldn't work either. Paul Harris would know right off who had started a police investigation at his home. But, I thought suddenly, what if I were right? Wasn't it worth the chance?

I answered that one easily enough — not for a minute. What I needed was a plan — a plan of action, some way to get into the Harris house myself and talk to Bethie, or

Terry. Yet how was I going to manage a thing like that?

I sat deep in thought. It was awful to feel so near a solution and not be able to think of one single way to begin finding out the truth.

I heated up some clam chowder for dinner, still thinking hard, and looking over at the Harris' house every once in a while, as if I would see something there that would help provide an answer.

And then, just as I was putting butter and croutons into the soup, I thought, "David!" and wondered where my mind had been up until now. Of course! I would tell him what I feared had been going on next door and David would help me. Why he was old Arlene's dear cousin. If anyone could get me into that house, David would be the one.

I started to eat happily. I would call David this evening and . . . but here my thinking jarred and stopped. I plunked the spoon down into my half-eaten chowder, my thoughts making me lose my appetite very quickly.

David? How could I possibly ask David? And now for the first time since I'd read the article in the paper, a chill swept over me, and for a moment I thought I was going to lose what little dinner I'd eaten. Was David involved in this too? I swallowed hard, fighting sickness, and forced myself to breathe deeply. How could I love him, and still wonder this way? I had many questions, but not the light of an answer.

I wrang my hands and washed the dishes and paced the kitchen, moaning aloud from time to time at my lack of total conviction that David was not, could not, be implicated. I also ached from the severing I was now so desperately afraid of. A cutting off from David, a knowledge that I had indeed picked the wrong person to love.

And then my thoughts switched back to little Bethie. What about her? What could I possibly do? I felt more lost and afraid and alone than I ever had before.

There was no answer. I only wanted to curl myself up in a tight ball, close my eyes, and not allow another horrible thought to creep into my mind.

CHAPTER
THIRTEEN

The next morning however, with the sun out and the sleet miraculously having vanished, I began to feel a little better. I would just keep thinking, as calmly and clearly as possible, and I would come up with an answer. I had to.

And then, in the early afternoon, something incredibly lucky happened. I had kept returning to the windows which overlooked the Harris', hardly knowing why I did this, but feeling a real need to stare out at their house, looking for an inspiration.

On one of these trips I saw the front door open and Paul and Arlene Harris come out. As I watched, they got into their car and drove away. Alone. They had not taken

Bethie with them. I looked at my watch. It was a little after one, which meant that Kate must still be at school.

Here was my chance! I dashed downstairs, grabbed a sweater off a hook by the door, and flew outside. There I slowed down. In case they decided to return for something, it would be pretty awkward for them to see me racing toward their house, or possibly even peering into windows.

I stood still and listened. It was quiet and windless out and strain as hard as I might, I could detect no sound of an automobile. Good. That meant I had a little time anyhow.

The air was cold and I regretted not having grabbed something heavier to wear, but I would lose precious time if I returned to the house now. I was making my way carefully and as quickly as possible over to the Harris'. I threaded my way from bush to tree to bush, and stopped every few seconds to listen, and I reached the side door in comparative safety.

I looked around me, half expecting the spook of Paul Harris to jump out with a cleaver and get me. But again all was late-fall silence, with a glittering sun sparkling the river and a high blue sky above me.

I turned the knob on the side door hopefully, but as I had expected, nothing happened. I also gingerly tried a few windows, but the ones I could reach were all locked too. I walked around to the side of the house, wondering what I should do next. How to get into that house and out of it before they returned home? And when would they be back anyhow? I wondered fearfully. Again I looked at my watch and was surprised to see that only ten minutes had passed.

I thought about calling out — if it were Terry and she were still up there, could she hear me through the boards? I supposed not, but decided to try anyhow — it was worth the chance.

I cupped my hands about my mouth, growing more and more fearful, and shouted up at the boarded windows, "Terry! Terry!"

My voice came back to my ears, reedy and thin-sounding. I stopped and coughed. Surely I could manage something louder? I tried again, but whether it was from fear or lack of conviction, I still couldn't get my voice to project. I kept choking on the name and finally had to give that idea up as one that just couldn't work for me now. There was no use my wasting time on trying to do something that my body just couldn't accomplish for me. I wondered at myself, wishing that I could have been braver, but not having the time now to chastise myself for cowardice.

I stood still to listen again, but no sound

came to my ears. And then I noticed the garage in back of the house. Its door was open and, as I had gotten nowhere yet, I decided to have a look inside. People put all kinds of things in their garages, didn't they? Maybe I would find something that would give me a hint of what to do next.

The garage proved to be a gold mine of confusion. Not a dead end, but a place I couldn't make any sense out of. In it were all kinds of children's toys and equipment. Mostly things too young to have been any good for Kate, and all of them looking old and used, beaten up and rusted. There was a crib and an old scummy tricycle, a few dolls, a baseball bat and glove, plus all sorts of other things, including a new shiny red fire engine and a huge carton pushed to the back of the garage, containing all kinds of ratty-looking baby and toddler clothes.

I stared at all this, fingering it with amazement. What did it mean? It looked like the Harrises did not just have Kate and Bethie, but a whole hoard of other children as well.

I lost all track of time, just looking, stupefied, trying to figure it out, when I heard the sound I had been straining for earlier. The noise of a car, growing nearer. I didn't move until I heard the crunch of tires on gravel, and then I was galvanized into action.

I was too deep into the garage to escape

without being seen, and having the Harrises find me out just now was something I couldn't possibly afford. I searched quickly around me, but the only possibility seemed to be the unwieldy carton of clothes. I pulled it forward and managed to sneak in behind it just as I heard the car stop.

Luckily I am quite slender, and so long as not a strand of my bright hair stuck out over the box, I thought I would probably be safe. But that knowledge, or hope, or whatever it was, did not stop me from living through a terrifying few minutes.

The Harrises hadn't driven right into the garage (I doubted if their car would *fit* anyhow), but stopped just short of it, and I was in a good spot to hear what they were saying. I crouched down as far as I could go and listened.

"She butts in aroun' here too much, Arlene. I tole you, I can't afford to have anymore a that." Paul's voice turned me to ice, as I realized I must be the subject of his remark.

"What's she gonna do anyhow?" was Arlene's unpleasant reply. "She can't do nothing!"

"I don' care," her husband growled, making me wince and shake in my hiding place. "I jus' don't want her around, hear?"

"Well, you don' suppose I *ask* her over here, do ya. She likes Kate, and the kid likes her."

"That's another one, our Kate," Paul accused. "Lot of help she's been to us lately. Firs' the thing with that miserable cat, and now she's all involved with what's-her-name next door."

"Oh, leave Kate be. She's all right," Arlene defended, and then: "Lissen, are you goin' to bring in some of those old clothes for the baby? She's been throwin' up and I can't keep up with the laundry. There oughta be some things in the garage that'd do."

My God! I thought, he's going to come in here and find me! I almost hugged the ground, trying to disappear. But there was nothing for me to do but be very still and pray I wouldn't be discovered.

"I'm not goin' in there now," Paul said, and I breathed a bit more easily until his next words: "You go get them if you need 'em so much," he finished, and I began trembling all over again.

"Oh, leave it till later," Arlene Harris said, a note of complaint in her voice. "I got to do everythin' around here by myself."

"So get Kate to help you. I tole you she's . . ." but then, thankfully and gratefully, their voices were lost to me as they turned toward the house.

I allowed myself to uncramp a bit, but waited a full five minutes by my watch before I dared push the carton away and

159

stand up. I sidled out of the garage and around it, going way to the back of the Harris' before I cut across to the safety of the Rinns' lawn.

So, I thought, going round the front of house and gaining the inside with relief and thanksgiving, they do have something to hide! And if they aren't kidnappers, then they're something else equally as bad.

I found that I was shaking like a puppy now, and went into the living room to turn up the heat and light a fire.

Huddling near the first splutterings of warmth, I went over the conversation I had just heard, remembering as much as possible.

Arlene Harris had referred to Bethie as the "baby." She was still sick, and neither one of them seemed to be involved in any way about her, which only substantiated what I had feared. But maybe, my thoughts were growing more and more mercurial, they were just uncaring parents? Yes, but then why would they not like me to be around? I rose to the challenge and answered myself: probably because they take lousy care of their kids and don't want anyone knowing it.

I dropped my head into my hands and squeezed against my temples. The problem was that I didn't know enough. Not nearly enough to make any really positive move.

I sat by the fire for a long time, just watching the flames and allowing my mind to wander unreined any way it would. I was exhausted, and still couldn't seem to get warm enough.

Out of the clutter and meanderings of my thoughts, at last I came up with the thing I must do next.

Wearily I dragged myself to my feet and headed for the hall. I couldn't go on with this by myself any longer. I had to take a chance.

I would call David.

CHAPTER FOURTEEN

This time I wasn't much concerned how David's voice would sound, whether he would be pleased to hear from me. The *fact* of him, my feelings, thinned in front of this horror next door that my imagination was so busy creating.

Of course it was not just my imagination, I reassured myself dialing. I had a whole network of feelings and reasons to support me. I did, didn't I? I questioned once again, hearing the phone ring.

My hand tightened on the receiver. David had to be home. Now that I had made the decision to ask for his help, I didn't think I could bear waiting another moment.

"Hello?" Thanks flowed freely from me when I heard his voice.

"David, hi." All of a sudden I was weak and trembly. I slid down to the floor, resting my head against the wall.

"Tanya! I was just thinking about you."

"Me too," I told him dully, "that's why I called."

"*I* know why you called," he said, but I could find no way of responding to the note of teasing in his voice.

"You do?" I asked weakly.

"You're a little late, but you called to invite me for Thanksgiving dinner. And even though you waited till the last minute, I accept."

"Thanksgiving?" I squeaked, "when's that?"

"Tomorrow, of course. And not for a moment do I believe that you've forgotten."

David was in fine spirits, I reflected, feeling anger rise in me and threaten to topple over.

"So. What time shall I be there?" he was asking as I fought for control. I couldn't wait until tomorrow. I could hardly wait another half hour. I needed David to come here right now. Thanksgiving? It buzzed in my head. My having forgotten told me just how absorbed I'd become lately.

"David, can you come over now?" I asked, brushing aside the holiday suggestion. After all, it was just not a time for celebrating.

"Oh, Tanya, honey, I'm sorry, but I can't. I'm driving into Boston tonight to give a lecture. At Boston U. Didn't I tell you about it?"

I shook my head dumbly, and then, realizing that of course he couldn't see me, I whispered, "No."

"It'll have to be tomorrow," David began, but I interrupted.

"Could you stop by after, David?" I was almost pleading now. "There really is something I need to talk to you about."

"I wish I could, but I'm not coming back till the morning, Tanya." His voice was regretful. "Some friends I haven't seen in years have asked me to stay the night."

"Oh." My voice was small and fuzzy. What could I do? There didn't seem to be any possibilities.

"Tomorrow, then?" David was prompting.

And I guessed that that was when it would have to be. There were no other choices open. I sat shaking on the floor, feeling as if I were tied up.

"Tanya?"

"Sorry, David." I cleared my throat and tried to sound all right. No sense in having him question me now; a telephone wouldn't do to explain. "Tomorrow will be fine. And

I must make you a dinner, must I?" I strove for a lightness that was hard for me to affect.

"A full *Thanksgiving* dinner," he underscored, "all the trimmings."

"You're lucky if you get a ham sandwhich," I replied, wondering idly if there was any bread in the house.

David laughed, which made me terribly upset. He thought I was kidding! He thought sweet little domestic housesitting Tanya really was going to whip him up a turkey with oyster stuffing and set the table with fine crystal and china. Well, no need to disillusion him yet.

"Two o'clock all right for you?" he asked.

"Fine, just fine," I answered, gently dropping the receiver in its cradle without bothering to say good-bye.

After I'd hung up, I sat still where I was and allowed a few tears to trickle down my cheeks. Everything was frustrating, and I was so trapped.

Curious, I lifted my arm to look at my watch. What time could it be? It seemed to me that days had passed since I was crouched down in the Harris' garage. I was shocked to see that it was only a bit after two. I held the watch up to my ear, but it was still ticking.

The empty day stretched in front of me,

promising no more than a deep, lasting depression. How could I just do nothing?!

My thoughts trailed slowly over the knowledge that it was Thanksgiving tomorrow. I remembered wonderful warm Thanksgivings with my parents — so good and filled with love that it made my throat ache now to recall them. But then I thought of the bleak holidays I'd spent with my aunt, and the ache turned to an anger at that woman who had understood nothing about me, and cared so little.

Then an idea came to me. I realized that I would need to keep busy till David got here tomorrow. Maybe it would be a good idea for me to make him that big dinner he'd done more than hint about. Not especially for David, because he'd coerced me, but as a therapy for myself. Yes, I decided, struggling up, it would be just the thing to keep me occupied, and tire me out so that I wouldn't think, wouldn't be able to.

I snatched the car keys from the hall table, put on a warm woolen jacket, and then, keeping my eyes carefully averted so that I would not be able to look over at the Harris', I drove carefully down the driveway and into town.

"Left your shopping for late, didn't you, Miss Sohier?" was Mrs. Collins' greeting. I nodded and smiled at her, too preoccupied filling my mind with food plans to stop for our usual chat.

I got back bursting with bundles and, dumping them down on the kitchen table, wondered if I really might be a little crazy. Here were awful things going on around me and I was about to make a feast worthy of James Beard at least. Maybe there's something wrong with your priorities, I told myself. But then I pushed all that away. I wouldn't, couldn't think now. Not till two o'clock tomorrow. Not till David came.

I spent most of the evening baking, preparing vegetables and stuffing, and setting an autumnal-looking Thanksgiving table. For the last I used a straw cornucopia I found in one of the kitchen closets, and filled it to overflowing with apples, nuts, and tangerines. Earth-colored dishes on a golden cloth and long white candles completed the picture. By one A.M., I was almost falling asleep on the floor.

The next morning I was up and about early, getting the turkey in and the cranberry pie baked.

Around eleven I decided to take a walk out back, away from the steamy kitchen whose lovely aromas were beginning to sicken me slightly. There is something heathen about Thanksgiving, I reflected, getting into a slicker against the misty day, all those piles of food and all that gorging. I sniffed appreciatively at the damp wet air.

"Happy Thanksgiving, Tanya." Kate, looking like a wood sprite in a rust woolen cloak and hood, poked her head through a bush to hail me.

"Kate!" My mind began to race, and all the things I'd hope to forget for just a few slim hours more came tearing back to me. But this was an opportunity too good to let easily slip by. It could do no harm for me to try and learn what I could from Kate. And the only approach, I realized, would have to be a fairly direct one.

"How's your little sister?" I asked as she emerged from the bushes. That had become one of my favorite questions lately.

"I don't know," Kate dug a foot into the moist earth, not looking at me. "Okay I guess."

"You mean better?" I prodded, but she just shrugged.

Maybe I was being too heavy-footed, I thought, and tried calming myself down for a new way in.

"I was wandering around the other day and saw all those toys and stuff in your garage, Kate," I said, flinging all caution into the river below me, and hoping she wouldn't read "wandering" for "spying."

"You and Bethie certainly have a lot of playthings." Tanya, you are a stinker, I rebuked myself, but Kate's startled reply was rewarding.

"They're not all ours," she said in surprise, and then her face paled a bit. She stepped back from me, and half turned, as if she thought of bolting.

"They're not?" I quickly feigned incomprehension. "Whose are they then?" Oh, don't leave, don't Kate, I sent silently out to her.

"Just other kids', I guess." I could see that she was feeling caught, and I shamelessly took advantage.

"You guess? Goodness! There are enough toys and clothes there to open a store." I walked closer to Kate. "There's nothing to be frightened of, honey," I laid a light hand on her shoulder, "I was just curious who all those things belonged to."

Kate looked around her. That furtive look I had so often noticed, almost a copy of her mother's. She opened her mouth as if she were about to speak, and then closed it again.

"Kate?"

She gave me a despairing look, but by now I was immune to what I might be putting her through.

"Tanya, if I tell you something, do you promise never to tell anyone else?" she asked. "I mean really promise?"

I nodded, wanting childishly to cross my fingers against the lie I was giving her. My heart began to thump, and I felt a strange excitement at getting close to what I'd been looking for.

"It's not really so important I guess," Kate went on, "only I'm not supposed to tell."

"I wouldn't hurt you, Kate," I said meaninglessly, but thinking that this, at least, was the truth. When everything began to get hairy next door, as I was sure now that it would, I would make sure, some way, that Kate was safely away from it all.

"My parents take care of kids sometimes, that's all," Kate said, leaving me in confusion.

"You mean baby-sit?" I asked, incredulous.

"Noo-o-o. More than that I suppose. My father works in this orphanage, and he sometimes brings kids home for a treat, kind of."

"Oh," was all I could think to say, while telling myself, so that's how they've explained it to her. And then I was struck by another thought. Kate had said "kids." Did that mean that they did this . . . this thing . . . often? I recoiled at the thought. And an orphanage . . . but I let that one go for now.

"Well, there's nothing wrong with that."
I strove to get the heavy tones out of my voice.

"No." Kate shook her head. "Only I'm not supposed to say."

"And I promise not to gossip," I told her, looking for words of truth so that later Kate would not confront me with anything like loathing.

She brightened. "Are you having a turkey?"

"I am. Are you?"

"Nope. Just a big chicken, but that's okay because my mother baked a cake. She hardly ever does that." Kate was smiling almost happily, and I thought with an awful wrench how little the Harrises gave, and what a small thing could please her.

Later, as I was checking the turkey which was just beginning to turn a crusty brown, it occurred to me that there was no vinegar in the house for the salad dressing.

After I'd gone inside and Kate had returned home, I had still practiced my non-thinking discipline. "Time enough later. There'll be time enough," I kept muttering to myself, skidding around the kitchen, making this meal much more difficult than it needed to be.

It was one-thirty, and I figured I had

time to pop into town and find an open grocery to buy some vinegar.

Not Mrs. Collins surely, I mused, going out to the car and remembering her rambling on about the huge meal she'd be cooking for Bridget and Julie, her two daughters who were bringing their husbands and children to Gloucester for the holiday.

When all this is over, I thought, starting the car and beginning to feel a bit uplifted, it will be wonderful to really live here again.

I put the car in reverse and pressed the accelerator, but nothing happened. The motor was running but the car wouldn't really start. It just churned sluggishly on the drive.

Oh murder, I thought getting out, what now?

As I walked around the car it was not difficult to see what was wrong. All my tires were flat — the air had been let out of them. I was obviously meant to know how coldly and purposely this had been done, because the air caps were set neatly on the ground, right beside each tire.

I stood looking down stupidly, thinking, oh, no, he didn't. And then I realized that of course there was no other explanation, and that yes, of course he had.

It had begun to rain more heavily now, and I hurried into the house. Well, I'll just use lemon instead of vinegar, I told myself strongly. It doesn't matter, it'll be all over soon and Paul Harris will be far too far away to get anywhere near me.

I was trying to sell myself a good story. It took me a little while to realize that the taste in my mouth was salt, and that I was crying.

CHAPTER FIFTEEN

I was upstairs, trying hastily to fix my face and unredden my eyes when I heard a car on the drive and flew to a window to make sure that it was David. It was.

I went downstairs to answer his knock, wondering again at the childishness, the immaturity of Paul Harris to pull a stunt like that. Of course he had succeeded in upsetting me badly and, I reflected, I suppose that was all he was after. For right now anyway. I wouldn't let my thoughts take me any further at the moment.

The sight of David was soothing, and I made myself hush any misgivings I might have about him. Here he was standing in my hallway, good and strong, carrying a bottle of Cold Duck for dinner. Someone I could depend on.

He kissed me briefly, just about eye-level, and then stood back. "Tanya, have you been crying?" he asked, and I could see worry crease thin lines on his forehead. Despite everything, I was extraordinarily pleased at his caring.

"No, of course not," I said, having decided to wait till I had a little turkey, yams, and wine in him to begin. I'd waited this long, I could wait an hour or two more. Besides, just having David here with me was a growing comfort. And the Harrises were eating at home, weren't they? I had time. "It's the oven, and that big dinner you made me cook for you." I laughed, taking the wine from him and going inside to stow it in the refrigerator.

David followed me. "Don't put that away. Let's have a glass of it before dinner," he suggested, "and I'll light a fire if you'd like me to."

"That'd be lovely, David," I said, warmth going through me. As I opened the wine and poured out two glasses of the sparkling red liquid, I told myself that I must wipe away any lingering fears I had about David's involvement. There was no way he could be, not David, I reaffirmed to myself, carrying the wine and some cheese into the living room.

"This house smells wonderful," David said, raising his glass in a toast to me.

"It ought to after the way I've been rushing about cooking and — "

"And of course you didn't even know it was Thanksgiving till yesterday." David grinned at me.

"I didn't," I admitted, sipping my wine.

David looked surprised. "You really didn't then? I thought you were kidding me, Tanya."

"No. I just forgot." I realized I was going to have to be very careful in order not to blurt everything out until after we'd eaten.

"How could you forget?"

"Oh, David, I don't know," I snapped. "The same way you keep forgetting to call me, I guess." That was out before I realized, and having said it, I got a good clue of how nervous I really was, and how much I kept pretending not to be.

"I think, my dear," David said in a chilly voice, "that you are not overly pleased to have me here."

He was sitting near the fire, his hands clasped about his knees, and I was aware of how much I liked his face. David was not really handsome, but craggy and strong looking. I was struck suddenly by the thought that I could go on looking at his face for years and years, and never grow tired of it.

"Don't be silly," I murmured to him, trying to smile in a way that would let him know how I felt.

He must have noticed something because his face began to relax and he leaned back, obviously comfortable, prepared to enjoy the day.

Seeing him so at ease made me restless. I put my glass down on the table and got up. "I'd better spend a little time in the kitchen, I think," I said, moving toward the doorway.

"Tanya?"

"Yes?" I stopped without turning around.

But David just repeated my name, forcing me to look at him. "What's wrong?" he asked gently.

"Wrong?" I tried to laugh, but only managed a brittle, cracking sound. "Nothing, David. Not anything really."

He looked at me closely. "But something, right? I was so involved about the lecture yesterday that — "

"And I didn't even ask you about it!" I said in dismay.

"That's not the point. What I started to say was that it wasn't till I was driving back from Boston today that I remembered how your voice sounded on the phone. All trembly, and today you're nervous as a cat. Tanya, sit down. You said you wanted to talk to me about something. What is it?"

Wow! I thought, losing my focus and grip for a moment, and strongly tempted to turn off the oven, sit down, and spill it all out.

But instead I shook my head. "No, David. Not now. You're right, I do want to talk to you about something. But later. After we've eaten, okay?" I'm not sure why I was insisting on this. I think it had something to do with an inner timetable I'd prepared for myself that I didn't want to change at the last minute. Perhaps it was a kind of superstition — if I did everything the way I planned I would, nothing would go wrong.

"It's up to you," David told me seriously. "You're sure?"

I nodded and, not trusting myself to stay a moment longer, went quickly into the kitchen where I began to bang around some pans. I put vegetables in serving dishes, carved the turkey, tossed the salad, and heated rolls in record time, and without quite knowing what I was doing. David came in and lounged in the doorway, watching me appreciatively.

"Even if I did talk you into this, I'm still glad I'm here," he said.

"Me too," I told him, brushing by with

platters to put on the dining-room table. "Very."

I think my dinner was a success. David seemed to get enormous enjoyment from it, but for my part I could eat next to nothing. What I did was to keep busy pushing food around on my dish so that he wouldn't notice and question me. I had managed a bite of turkey, which tasted like cardboard, and some brussels sprouts that had a definite pasty flavor. But as David's talk was filled with compliments, I thought it must be me and not the food.

David helped me clear the table and I suggested that we have coffee and pie by the fire.

He winced. "I don't think I could manage another bite."

"Not even a slice of hot buttery cranberry pie?" I coaxed.

"If you force me." He looked around the kitchen which was filled with messy dishes and food. "Would you rather get a start on these dishes first?"

There was of course nothing I would rather not do. My control was unraveling fast, and I would easily have broken all the dishes and thrown them away rather than even begin to think of taking the time now to wash them.

"No, let's just leave all this," I managed, setting a tray with the pie and coffee.

"I guess I'm too lazy right now anyhow," David said, easily giving in.

We settled in the living room, and I was aware, suddenly, of what a comfortable picture the two of us made — legs tucked up on the couch, cat snoozing by the fire, warm mellow light, hot coffee and pie — a house-beautiful scene. It was just too bad that it wasn't true, I thought sadly.

I took a sip of my coffee but it tasted burned and I set the cup onto the saucer with a clink.

David looked over at me. "Come on, give," he said, and like a shot I uncurled myself and sprang for the desk where I'd put the clipping from the paper.

Silently, I handed it to David and watched his face as he read. But his expression, unchanging, told me nothing. Finally he looked up. "Is this it, Tanya? Is this what you wanted to talk to me about?"

I nodded, fearful of trusting my voice.

"It's awful, I know," David went on. "I saw it in the paper myself, but I don't see why — "

"It's them, David! It's the Harrises! They have Terry, I'm sure they do." I heard myself, excited but steady-sounding. Only my hands, which I held clamped in my lap, would have given me away. If I unloosed them and they began shaking all over the place, I was sure David would just label me "hysteric."

For a moment he remained quiet, and when he did speak, I was totally unprepared. "You can't be serious about this, Tanya."

I was stunned. Was David going to shut me out so completely? Not even find out why I felt so positive. Wasn't he going to ask me any questions at all?

But it seemed that he was not. Or at least not just yet. I gathered all the courage I had left and went on to talk to him as calmly as possible, outlining, detailing for him, filling in all the things I'd left blank when we'd had dinner together. And I went further than that — telling him what had happened since that night, my conversations with Kate and my encounters with her parents, even to my hiding in the garage. Finally letting him know as completely as I could why I believed the Harrises were holding a kidnapped child next door.

I watched his face carefully as I spoke, but all I could see there was concentration. Finally I paused, wondering what I had left out, what I could add.

But David spoke before I could think of anything else. "Tanya, I can see why you're upset — "

"Upset!" I exploded. "It's a lot more than

that! David, haven't you taken anything I've just told you seriously?"

"Of course I have. And as I said, I see why you're upset, but I'm sure you've made a mistake." He shook his head. "The whole thing is just too fantastic."

"Don't you think I know that? And that I've been suffering over all kinds of doubts myself before I brought all this to you?"

"I'm sure you have. But you've been here alone so much. You've allowed your mind to run away with you, I think, to create all kinds of nightmares." He put his hand on my arm and tried to draw me toward him. "It's been terribly unpleasant for you, honey," he said, "and there's no doubt that Paul Harris is a monster. I'd like to get my hands on him for the way he's treated you, but — "

"Don't, David," I told him, pushing away and shaking his arm off me. I was in no state to be cajoled like a child after a bad dream. "I'm perfectly serious about this, and if you think it's all foolish, then never mind!" It wasn't the strongest thing I could have said to him, but at the moment I was not feeling especially coherent or verbal.

"Tanya, give me a little while to think it over, will you?" David asked, and I wanted to swat him. What, after all, was there to think over? He just wanted to figure out a gentler way to tell me he thought I'd gone off half crazy. Just one of your everyday illogical females!

I was fuming, too angry now to even listen to what else he was saying to me. And then I had a thought. My car! If I showed him the tires, maybe that would jolt him.

"Come with me, David, I want to show you something." I was aware that I sounded like an army sergeant, but I was way past caring about anything like that now.

David followed me outside and inspected my tires. "And you think Paul Harris did this?" he asked, looking up at me.

"Not think, David! Know! I know he did it." I realized that my voice was rising and bordering on tears. I also knew that if I had any hope at all of trying to convince David, I should remain calm. But I just couldn't do it. I was too strung out and there was no way back for me to try and collect myself.

"Kids do this kind of thing all the time, Tanya. It's a prank, that's all." He rose and I was dismayed to see the tenderness in his eyes. The rotter is feeling *sorry* for me, I thought, boiling with indignation.

"I'll speak to Arlene about Paul, though," he said, putting an arm around my shoulder. "She's a little dim herself, but

I'm sure she could do something to stop him from bothering you. I don't mean about the tires, though. I'm positive he couldn't have had anything to do with that. But you don't have to live in fear because there's an illiterate drunk living next door to you."

I moved away from David's arm, going slowly out of his reach. "Thanks, but don't bother, David," I told him. I hadn't any more energy to expend trying to convince him. He'd let me down terribly. Treated me like an overexcited child. Not for a moment did he consider that my suspicions might be justified.

Back in the house I yawned elaborately and turned to him. "Do you mind, David? I'm just so very tired." What I needed now, badly, was for him to leave.

"Listen, Tanya, let me — "

"Please, David. Really. I've got to be alone now. I don't want us to talk anymore."

Obediently, to my surprise, he slipped on his coat. Then he took my shoulders in his hands and gave me a soft shake. "Hey, you." I raised my eyes to meet his. "You be all right, huh? I'll call you in the morning, we'll talk some more."

"Okay," I whispered, hardly taking in his words, vaguely feeling his lips brush mine.

And then David was gone, and I stood

in the doorway alone, with the black night eclipsing the trees and lawn, creeping in to wash over me as the first spray of rain and wind wooshed through the hallway and echoed in the rooms.

CHAPTER
SIXTEEN

I thought I'd better try to make some sense
out of the kitchen, knowing all the time
that it was either do that or hide in my bed
and cry out all my loneliness, hurt, and frustration. I opted for work. Even though I
didn't like knowing that I was using my
aunt's remedy, I felt if I didn't do something, I definitely would go crazy.

Everything was a mess: gluey gravy,
limp vegetables congealed in butter, scraps
of turkey and stuffing on the counter, on
the plates, on the table, and even some on
the floor, which Peabody was busily cleaning up for me.

I knelt down beside him, brushing my
face against his fur and kissing him.

"You're my best friend," I whispered, but Peabody moved aside in annoyance to finish the job he'd set himself.

I almost wailed at his rejection but stopped myself and began scraping and piling things. As I worked I made no conscious effort to keep David or our conversation away — it wasn't necessary. My mind just didn't go in that direction. Instead I was caught up thinking about a bunch of practical, everyday things — getting the car fixed, buying cat food, visiting a gallery that had opened in town. All these little matters occupied me and I was grateful that they did. I knew that hiding underneath, the hurt was waiting to leap out and gobble me up. If I felt anesthetized for a few hours I might gather some strength to handle that pain when it came.

I knew too, with a part of my mind, that I must now disregard David as being any help to me with the Harrises or, I acknowledged, with anything else, in anyway else. But that could not stop *me*. My thoughts and fears had committed me to some kind of action, and as soon as I could clear my head I would figure out for myself what I must do.

I knew then that David's attitude hadn't moved me an inch. My own determinations had not wavered because of his write-off, his rationalizations. Everything next door was not peachy, that was something I was positive of. They were hiding Terry and masquerading her as Bethie. David would not face that because — but here I got bogged down in my thinking. I couldn't get over the because part, which made me stop wrapping up the leftover turkey for the freezer and consider.

Why had David so blithely pushed aside everything I'd told him? Of course he did tell me that he needed time to think, but I didn't believe that for a moment — he just said that as a stall, to stop me from pouring out any more of my fantastic thoughts to him.

But why? I badgered myself wondering and trying to understand. I completely stopped what I was doing and sat down at the table to try and make some sense out of it. This, at least, wasn't painful, it was just regular practical thinking that I needed to do before I could make my next move.

It probably took so long for me to figure it out because I just flatly didn't want to. I was pushing some spilled sugar around in a crazy pattern on the tablecloth when there was a leak in my mind, and knowledge came flowing, flooding through. A painful, ugly realization that made me feel as if the table were moving away from me and the room spinning around.

In a few moments, when everything had sort of settled back into place, I was able to put words to my thoughts, and then haltingly to even make a sentence: Obviously David was mixed up with Paul and Arlene Harris, and very naturally he didn't want my suspicions, not to mention my interference. Of course this thought had passed through my mind before, but never, deep down where I lived, had I actually believed it.

I got up abruptly, heavy with this new knowledge, and almost needing to find a place where I could push it, squeeze it in, just to hide it away. I headed for the living room to collect our coffee things, knowing all the time that there was no brushing anything aside now.

It was awful and terrible and made me shake with a kind of aching emptiness, and also a curious feeling of fury. I'd been so thoroughly duped! And by somebody I'd thought I was in love with. Somebody whom, I acknowledged, slamming plates onto the tray, I was probably *still* in love with.

I carried everything back into the kitchen, wondering how I could even begin to think that I was possibly still in love with David.

I pushed the dishes into the hot water

and began scrubbing them vigorously. Well, at least the kitchen was almost clean, I told myself with no satisfaction. I had only to finish up with the dishes and put away the cranberry pie.

The pie! Well of course, I thought suddenly. Why *not* use the pie? It would be as good an excuse as any.

All of a sudden I was terribly excited. I did a bad job with the rest of the dishes and, not giving myself a moment to think, I hastily wrapped the remainder of the cranberry pie up in tin foil. I would bring Kate some Thanksgiving dessert, and I would not leave that house until I'd managed to find out something very definite, a clue (and even in my unruly state I had to laugh at the dramatics of that word) that would allow me some concrete evidence against the Harrises. And then I would return home and calmly call the police because I could not go on with this by myself any longer.

I went around to the side door of their house, knowing I would get no response in front.

As I stood shivering in the wet air, it occurred to me that my knock might not bring any answer here either. But the door opened almost immediately and Paul Harris' bulky frame was before me. He was in shadow and I could not read his face, so I plunged into busy conversation. Before he could make a move to stop me, using the distraction of my words as a wedge, I slipped past him into the house.

"Happy Thanksgiving," I babbled. "I've just realized that I had all this cranberry pie left over and I thought maybe you would enjoy it. Have you finished eating yet? I hoped I'd be in time for your dessert." As I spoke I headed for the kitchen where, from the dishes piled up in the sink, I could see that dinner was indeed over.

"Who is it, Paul?" Arlene's voice called from another room, and then I dared to turn around and look Paul Harris directly in the face.

"It's our neighbor," he yelled to his wife, giving the word an unpleasant taste, his ominous expression making me quail for a moment. In fact I almost dropped the pie on the nearest unoccupied surface and tried to make a run for it. But I'd gotten myself this far, I just couldn't be a coward now.

"Where's Kate?" I chattered on as Arlene came into the room. "I thought I might wish her a Happy Thanksgiving."

They both stood looking at me, saying nothing, until Arlene muttered, "She's busy now. What do ya want?"

I indicated the pie with my hand. "Just

to drop off some pie for her, and for both of you," I thought to add. My mind was galloping. I had to act quickly now, or the very least they would do was throw me right out of the house.

"How's your daughter?" I asked, in a voice that came out almost as a demand. Although I could hardly tell, my heart was beating so loudly it was difficult to hear anything over it.

Arlene Harris looked confused for a moment. "I jus' tole you Kate was busy. She's okay, she's busy."

I swallowed hard. "I don't mean Kate," I said, spacing my words carefully now because I was finding breathing difficult. "I mean Terry." And then I immediately covered my mouth with my hand — a very stagey gesture — and went on to add: "Oh, but of course, you call her Bethie, don't you?" I shook my head. "That was a dumb mistake to have made. I meant Bethie, of course. How is she?"

At this Paul Harris took a step forward and lurched against a chair. I looked over at him quickly, realizing with a sick sinking in my stomach, that he was very, very drunk.

For the next few moments, everything happened in a rush — almost like watching an old-time movie flickering on the screen. Arlene reached a hand out to tug at her husband's sleeve, but he pulled angrily away from her to stand tall and awful-looking right in front of me. His face was just inches from my own so that I could smell the liquor and sourness coming from him. I moved back a step, prepared to stand my ground and repeat my question, but Paul grabbed me by the shoulders and raised me up till my eyes were staring directly into his. I noticed how swollen and bloodshot his eyes were.

"What da you want over here, huh?" He shook me until I thought that if he continued I would go limp all over and be totally useless. And then he was mumbling something under his breath that I couldn't make out, and Arlene was pulling at his arm again and talking to him in what sounded like an imploring voice.

I couldn't really tell because my head had begun to buzz and I was sure that at any moment I would faint.

Then, without warning, I was being pushed down a dark hallway. There seemed to be noise and confusion all around me, but I was trying, fighting too hard to keep conscious to be aware of much of it. I did make out Paul saying, "I'll show you . . . I'll fix you," or something like that, and again Arlene's voice, pleading with him — I suppose to let me go.

At the end of the hallway was a flight of

stairs and he shoved me toward them roughly, so that I had no choice but to climb on my wobbly, spaghetti-legs, his hand on the middle of my back bracing me, urging me forward.

At the top of the stairs a door flew open, revealing a lighted room, into which I was thrust, so hard that I toppled and fell down, grazing my knees on the wooden floorboards.

I heard the thud of the door crashing closed behind me at the same time as Kate's voice screamed my name.

CHAPTER
SEVENTEEN

In a few seconds I began to collect myself.
The buzzing in my head lessened and I
pushed my body into a sitting position.

Kate was cowering in a corner, a look
of fear on her face. Was it me? Was Kate
afraid of me? I pushed the hair out of my
eyes and moved my body, just to make
sure that I was still able to.

There wasn't much in the room besides
Kate: a small metal dresser, a wooden coat
stand, and, oddly enough, a rubber doll with
blonde hair, lying over near the dresser. I
was just about to make myself get up and
go over to Kate when, from the corner of
my eye, I saw another object. A large one
with bars on it. It took me a moment — I

guess my mind was still foggy — to realize that it was a crib. When I finally identified it, I had a sensation like walking into unbearable cold water.

"Tanya! Are you all right? Please! Please talk to me, look at me!" But Kate's voice was coming from a great distance. My eyes were rooted to the crib. I couldn't, I just could not make myself turn and look at her, see if she were still pressed into that corner. Neither could I find my voice to answer her. I would worry about Kate later, soon. Now I had to manage to get to that crib and look inside it. I was terrified and for moments seemed actually incapable of any movement at all.

At last I moved forward a few steps, and then it got easier and I managed finally to stand up and walk over to the crib. I felt as if I were walking on marshmallows, but I made it to the crib and put out a hand to steady myself against it.

I looked down, into the thin, sleeping face of a little girl, probably about four or five years old. Her color wasn't good, and, as I stared I saw how shallow her breathing was. She lay there so still and quiet. A spasm of fear shook me. Just at a time when I would have thought it impossible for me to know a deeper terror, I realized that I had found one. The child looked like she was dying! I don't know how I knew that, but I sensed it strongly and I was not about to argue that fear away.

I gripped the edge of the crib, waiting for strength to ease back to me. And then I turned, almost in slow motion, to Kate, who had moved away from the wall and was edging toward me.

"What is it? What's wrong with her?" I asked in a voice little above a whisper. But at least I was able to speak again.

"Nothing . . . I don't think." I could now easily see Kate's nervousness and fear.

"Kate." My voice was louder now, stronger. "Is this Bethie? Your sister?"

Wordlessly, she shook her head, gazing down at the floor.

"It's Terry, isn't it?" I asked her, marveling at my calmness.

But as she heard my words, Kate's head shot up and she looked at me in complete surprise. A small frown gathered on her forehead. "What do you mean, Tanya? It's Bethie. Not Terry. There's no Terry."

"Come here, Kate," I said, and she did. "Now don't lie to me. This is terribly important. Do you realize that your father almost . . . that he — "

"No, don't, Tanya, please!" Kate's voice caught in a sob. "I know, I saw him. I don't know why . . . are you all right?" She reached out a hand and tentatively touched my arm. And at that I pulled Kate to me and hugged her hard, feeling a nice warmth, the first, I realized, that I'd felt in a long time, flow between us.

"Don't worry. I'm fine, Kate, just a little shaky right now. But honey, you have to tell me . . . about her, about the baby." I couldn't bring myself to tell Kate that her parents were kidnappers. I had no idea what stories they'd been telling her, but whatever she'd have to be told about them must be done in a gentle way — not a sudden exposure from me right now.

Kate gave a huge sigh. "It's Bethie," she said, looking down with me into the crib. "She's sick, I think. My parents got her some stuff, and they thought she was getting better, but this afternoon she began crying all over again and then my father gave her some more medicine. To make her sleep and stop whimpering. He sent me up here to watch out for her." Kate looked up at me, puzzled. "She's been sleeping like this for hours. She hasn't even moved hardly."

I felt my body tighten. The baby must be drugged, but Kate couldn't know that. Somehow, before it was too late, I would have to get help.

And then, the windows! I thought. Maybe I could manage to get out that way. My mind recalled the rasp of a key in a lock just after I'd been thrown into this room.

I was being kept a prisoner of sorts for a while, but I'd figure a way out. I had to. Even as I was thinking, I ran to a window, and pushed the shade aside. Had I thought about it I would have known. Of course! These were the windows I'd seen Paul Harris boarding up. My eyes met glass and strips of blank rough wood with not even a chink between them. It would be useless to try and escape this way.

"Kate." I turned and walked slowly back to the crib. "You said this wasn't your sister. Tell me who Bethie is then, and tell me why she's here." I stuck with the "Bethie." It was easier surely for Kate, and somehow, I realized as I spoke, for me too.

I could see that Kate was very uncomfortable again, but I could also tell that she was going to answer me, and that what she said would be the truth.

Her words came out in a rush, but they were succinct, with no embellishments. "Remember, I told you my father works at an orphanage, Tanya, and that sometimes he brings a baby or a little kid home so my mother can take care of it, give it a better place to stay until the orphanage finds a home for it. We've had a lot of kids here, but none of them have ever gotten sick before." She looked over at the crib, worry making her small face tight.

I stared at her in amazement. This was

what she'd really been told! My mind recoiled from the fact that there had been
others, who could even guess how many
others. Right now it was this one child that
had all my concern.

I turned away from Kate and began to
walk about the room, trying to think, to
find a way out of this for all of us.

And just then a sound reached my ears.
It was the gunning of a motor. Somewhere
below us a car was being started. I stood
very still, straining to hear. The sound
grew clearer, and I could discern, faintly,
the rush of gravel against tires. Quickly
I ran from one window to the next, hoping
for a peephole in one of the boards. There
were none.

"Kate!" I cried, "they're leaving! Your
parents are leaving and we're shut up in
this room."

"I know," she nodded. "That was really
dumb of my father, to lock the door, I
mean. I don't know why he did that, except
. . . I think, I guess he's been drinking."

I could not believe her calmness, her
obvious lack of fear. I reached to get my
voice down where it wouldn't sound so
shrill. "Do you know where they're going?"
I asked her evenly, my mind flashing with
pictures of ransom notes, money being
left. . . .

"I think they were supposed to go pick

up the people who're going to adopt Bethie. Or meet them somewhere or something," she told me, and then she must have noticed the fear painted all over my face. "Don't worry, Tanya. It'll be okay. When they come back, Daddy'll let you out." She giggled. "This is really silly, isn't it?" she asked me. "Our being locked up here, like princesses in a castle or something."

At that moment I very much envied Kate her innocence. It would be nice to laugh and feel part of a fairy tale for a little while.

And then, just as I was beating at my mind for a way to escape, uselessly trying the door which was unbudgeable as cast-iron, again the sound of a car floated up to me.

"Did you hear that, Kate?"

She looked at me, confused. "No, what?"

But try as hard as I could, I could not follow the sound. It seemed to have stopped. "I thought I heard a car," I said, feeling, for some reason, sheepish.

"Oh, they couldn't be back already, Tanya. They just left," Kate explained, as if she were speaking to a child.

I subsided, thinking maybe I really had made it up. And then I knew I hadn't. Below us I could hear a dull pounding, as if someone were trying to get into the house.

Whoever it was, I thought crazily, would be very welcome. I ran to a window and began pounding on it to let the person down there know that someone was up here. Trapped up here, I thought giddily now that rescue seemed preciously close.

"Tanya! Don't do that! You don't even know who it is. Besides my father wouldn't want anyone coming in now," Kate pleaded with me, but I paid no attention to her. Kate had no idea what was going on.

In a few minutes whoever it was had evidently gotten into the house. I heard thudding footsteps on the stairs, and then I began to yell. "Up here! We're up here!" I shouted over and over again, not paying any attention to the fear and surprise on Kate's face.

I watched fascinated as the door began to shake, rattle on its frame, and then, finally, when I thought I could bear it no longer, heave in and swing forward, hanging from its hinges.

David stood, disheveled and panting in the doorway. And, seeing him, I knew a moment of complete panic. I grabbed Kate and pushed her behind me, using both of our bodies to shield the crib.

"Tanya!" David shouted, seeing my face.

"Get out of here. Leave us alone," I cried, pressing both Kate and me hard into the crib's bars.

I knew that there was little chance of David's leaving, but if he would, if he only would then I could get Kate and the baby out of the house. The Rinns had the other car, I could use that, drive into town for help. . . . All these pictures flashed across my mind, including a lovely one of the new brick and glass police station on Main Street. . . .

David took a few steps into the room.

"Tanya, what is it? What's the matter with you?"

"Don't pretend with me any longer, David." I tried hard to sound nasty, but my voice kept giving after every word. "If you do a thing, just one little thing to harm Kate or this child — " and here my voice broke completely for a moment.

"What are you talking about?" David demanded in an ugly voice, and I wondered how long he was going to try to keep up this pretense.

"This child is sick, David. Terribly sick! Did they even bother to tell you that? Or didn't you care?" I tried hard for a bravado I didn't feel. If he could believe that I wasn't afraid of him, maybe I'd have a chance.

David began to talk to me slowly and softly, as if he were reasoning with someone not responsible, a little goofy. "If the baby's sick, Tanya, wrap her up and we'll take her to the hospital. You don't want to just leave her lying there if she's not well."

"No, I don't!" I shot back at him, "But I'm not getting in any car with you either! Now you get out of here, do you hear me, you — "

"Kate," David interrupted. "Is Bethie really sick?"

"Yes," Kate mumbled, slipping out a little from behind me to answer. "But my parents'll be back soon, and they'll — "

"Hush, Kate," I cautioned her, fearing that she would tell David — what? I wasn't really sure. But I knew I didn't want either of us to give him any information.

As I turned my head to look back at the baby, who was, I saw, still breathing in that forced, labored way, David came up next to me. I felt his nearness as air moving next to me, and I screamed a high, thin scream and lashed out at him with my hands, my arms, with any part of my body that would work at all, to push his threatening presence away.

And then, with a spasm of pain, I felt my arms being pinned down at my sides and my head began to throb with the awful shaking it was getting. I heard Kate cry out and then I felt a strong blow on the side of my face which sent me reeling backwards. It was as if I were tumbling, falling. I saw David's eyes. The only real things in the room. They seemed to be flickering sparks at me. Or was that my eyes?

And then I was tumbling again, falling
through some great space as if I had
stumbled down the rabbit's hole and were
about to surface in Eat-Me Land.

I thought I could hear David and Kate
both calling my name, but I wasn't really
sure of that. I was weightless, buoyant. And
then, abruptly, darkness slipped over me
like a hangman's blind.

CHAPTER
EIGHTEEN

I came around to a sensation of cold and dampness. My head felt as if it were being squeezed between two rocks, and I opened my eyes to a twilight where everything discernible looked fuzzy and strange. I had no idea where I was, and for a moment I couldn't remember why I should be anywhere that was strange.

I tried to make myself think, but it was so terribly difficult with the pounding in my temples and the feeling that part of my face had come unstrung, that I closed my eyes again and began drifting back to sleep.

But somehow I couldn't find that thick, floating blackness I'd just surfaced from. As I lay suspended somewhere between sleep and wakefulness, miniscule images kept forming in my head in little spurts that forced sleep back. The trouble was that I could make no sense of them — a wide mouth screaming in pain, fair hair matted with dried blood, a room with bars on the window and a figure trying desperately to pull them apart. ...

I snapped to full consciousness with a start, as memory came back to me. I opened my eyes once more and this time the room came fully into focus. Light yellow walls dimmed by a gray rain, light maple furniture, a Van Gogh print — and then, slowly, my eyes slewed round, and I found David, sitting upright, tense, in a chintz-covered armchair.

I opened my mouth to scream, but only managed to utter a rusty-sounding croak. As I pushed myself up on my elbows, kicking, trying to free myself from the bedclothes, a severe dart of pain shot through my head, making jagged colored lines appear before my eyes.

"Don't! Tanya, darling, please lie back." David's voice pierced through the haze of pain.

I moaned and sank against the cool pillows as David approached me, forcing a glass of water against my lips. With a strength I would have doubted I possessed, I slammed my hand against the glass sending it spinning out of David's grasp, water splashing on his arm and the comforter. Surprise, and what looked like a kind of hurt, swept over his face.

"Kate," I rasped out, "Bethie, where — "

"They're fine. They're both all right, Tanya, really, you mustn't worry."

"Where are — "

"They're safe. They're going to be fine. I have Kate — "

"You?" I struggled to sit up, tried again against the thumping pain.

But this time David just laid a strong hand on my shoulder and pushed me back onto the bed. I fought weakly, but the pressure of his arm remained, and, finally, I had to give up, resigned for the moment that I was in no condition to match David, physically at least.

"I hit you, Tanya, and you fell. Your head struck the side of the crib. The doctor says it's a slight concussion and you must stay quiet." David spoke matter-of-factly.

My thoughts spun in circles: The doctor? David had called the doctor for me? Was he telling me the truth? I looked at him closely. He'd sat back down again, his hands hanging limp between his knees. But why would he lie to me now? unless he were planning to kill me or something, I thought giddily, realizing that if he killed me there would be no "or something" left. I felt a sudden desire to laugh, but I knew it would hurt too much. I felt extremely tired and unreal, and thought that they — someone — must have given me some medication, a drug to make me feel this way.

"What's happening?" I questioned David, needing desperately for him to tell me, praying that I'd believe him.

David sighed and ran his fingers through his hair, which left him looking disheveled and boyish — the words sprang to my mind, but I pushed them back, they hinted at a tenderness I no longer felt for him.

"You're supposed to rest. You're not supposed to get excited," he told me, saying the words as if they were memorized, instructions he'd been cautioned to carry out.

"Rest!" I let my eyes plead with him. "David I've got to *know*! How can you expect — "

But he put up a hand to silence me. "All right, all right, Tanya. I'll tell you a bit so you can stop worrying. But just be still, will you?"

I swallowed around the huge basketball that had just formed in my throat. Unable to get out a sound, I nodded at him slightly, but even that small movement made the pain once more tear across my eyes.

"Let me tell you first," David said, "just for myself, that I am not now nor have I ever been involved in any way with my cousin and her husband." He grinned at me feebly. The legalese was a mild attempt at a joke I supposed, to lighten the situation. I did not smile back.

"As I told you before, Kate and Bethie are both fine, really." His eyes held mine, deep and hard for a moment, and though I struggled with it, I finally, haltingly, was able to believe at least this.

"By the way it *is* Bethie, not Terry," David went on. "You were wrong about that — about the kidnapping thing, I mean." He looked down, studying the hooked rug on the floor as if it were a wounded animal, and then he shook his head slowly. "But you weren't wrong about much else. I was so blind, Tanya. I just kept my head in the sand. I didn't realize, I couldn't believe. . . . Anyhow," he caught himself up, "you were right that there was denitely something wrong next door."

I was in an agony of suspense. If David didn't get on with it soon, I'd get out of this bed somehow and bash his skull in!

"The thing is," David said, seeming to read me, "that Paul and Arlene were dealing in something that's very like black-market babies, only in their case a lot nastier. Kate said she'd told you her father worked in an orphanage. Well, that part's true enough. What *isn't* true is that out of a sense of kindness and humanity they took kids from the home in, to give them a kind of family feeling of security, love even." David laughed bitterly before he continued. "Paul had quite a few unsavory connections, nothing really to do with the orphanage, I don't think. Anyhow, he got into this racket by finding out, discovering in some way, parents who had at some time been accused of maltreating their children. We don't know yet how he found out about these people. It'll come out eventually, but that's not the important part. It's what he did with his knowledge, how he — " David paused, looking away from me, out the window. I thought that if I didn't bring him back quickly, I would burst.

"David. Please," I choked, urging him on with my eyes.

"Sorry," he said shortly, and turned back to me so that I could read the pain on his face. He cleared his throat. "Anyhow, most of these parents that he approached were people who had been played upon before — terrorized even. Paul Harris used them, leveled another blow at them by using their children to threaten them. What he did was fairly simple. These people had been to court before over some problem with their children. Most of them had been found innocent, but that didn't matter so much to them — they'd already been terrified by having been subpoenaed. Harris got to them and threatened to tell the police that they'd once again been misusing their children. Well, most of them believed him. None of it was true, of course, but they believed him because they were scared, because most of them had no money and were struggling just to feed another mouth.

"It took a little time, but Paul was clever. He managed well. When he had them thoroughly frightened, he offered them some money. Not a great deal I'd guess, but probably a sum that seemed like a lot to them. He offered it to them for their child, and also to buy *his* silence. In almost every case they gave in.

"Paul and Arlene then took the child home with them, gave it what even you could see was minimal care, and then Paul made arrangements to sell the child to some family the orphanage had turned down as being unqualified. Babies, even young children, are hard for people to come by if an orphanage hasn't found a couple satisfactory, and so Arlene and Paul made quite a little money on these flesh deals."

David stopped for a few minutes to give me time to try and take it in. I felt tears prick my eyelids for all those babies, those children who could probably never be traced now, living with people who had been turned down as not being fit.

Suddenly I had a picture of Arlene Harris leaving the house one night all bundled up. . . . I'd seen it, watched from my window as she'd taken one of those children out, to deliver to someone . . . like a side of beef . . . a child, that way.

Then David was holding me in his arms and I was crying, tears washing down over my face, my head throbbing.

"Shhhh, hush, honey, it's all right now," David soothed, pressing my head to him, untangling the snarls in my hair, and whispering gently to me.

"How," I finally got out, "how did you find all this out so quickly?"

David let go of me, easing me back down against the pillow. I looked up to see him grinning broadly at me. "Not as quickly as all that. You've been unconscious, or just semiconscious for the last three days, Tanya. Paul and Arlene are in custody, Kate's here in my house, and Bethie's in the hospital." Then, at my look of fear, "No, she's going to be fine. Honestly. They've found her parents, and they're looking after her."

A breath of relief passed through me. At least I'd accomplished that much. I'd helped save Bethie.

"If Paul hadn't been so drunk on Thanksgiving night, he'd never have put you up in that room with Bethie. I don't know, I don't even want to think what he planned to do with you when they got back.

They'd had to leave to make arrangements about getting rid of the child. But Paul probably believed he could badger you, scare you in some way. I don't know," David said.

I shivered under the thick coverings. I didn't want to think about it either.

"Things were getting a little hot for them in Boston, that's why they moved out to Gloucester. They thought it would be a better cover for them." David's eyes glowed at me. "I guess they just hadn't figured on moving right next to the neighborhood snoop!"

"The — ? Why you — "

"Uh, uh, not now," David said, flipping the hand I'd tried to swat him with right back to me. In spite of my pounding head and all that had been going on around me, I began to feel better. Warmth was coming back. David's caring was near and had a good feeling.

But then I thought of all the questions that hadn't been answered, and I mentally pushed the comfort of David away from me for a little while yet. "David?" I was tentative, remembering the coldness I'd found in him, how he had been able to erase me with a word or a look. But now we needed to have something firm to build on; and I dismissed any fear I had of his reaction and went on: "David, why did you keep going over to see them?"

214

He looked puzzled for a moment. "I didn't keep going over."

"Twice?"

"Twice, that's all." He laughed at me. "Tanya, you really do have the makings of an incredible busybody." But he stopped laughing quickly. I think we were both terribly aware of each other, and we had to keep rerealizing that there was no room, just yet, for laughter, or for touching.

"I went the first time only to see Arlene for a few moments because I hadn't known until then that they had moved into town. I don't know why Arlene even bothered to get in touch with me, although I expect it had something to do with my medical acumen."

"Your what?" I didn't know where he was going.

"No, really," David insisted. "I know that sounds weird, but I went to see them the second time on Arlene's invitation. She apparently wanted to talk to me quite badly. And then when I got there, Paul was home and she seemed very uncomfortable. She told me that they had this foster daughter, Bethie, and that she was ill. I didn't really take much notice of it at the time, but just the other day I realized that she wanted help, or information, or something like that from me. They couldn't risk taking the child to a doctor and having a lot of questions asked, so I guess Arlene decided that a vet was better than nothing. And then Paul turned up, and she didn't want him to see that she was trying to coax information out of me. She was so subtle about it that I didn't even realize what she'd been trying to do till just a short while ago."

I listened to David's words with satisfaction. It all made sense, including his not wanting to get involved with the Harrises, or hear any stories about them. David, like me, had sensed that there was something wrong, but he hadn't wanted to face it. He'd been right, he *had* been an ostrich, and I guessed that just now he was feeling a little ashamed of himself. Should I pour a little salt? I played with the idea for seconds, but rejected it as being a very unworthy thing to do to both of us.

"What made you come back, then?" I asked him, "on Thanksgiving, I mean."

"You did," he answered promptly. "All the way home, I couldn't get you and what you'd told me out of my mind. I admit I didn't think that there was much truth in your theories, but somehow I was frightened for you, for what you might try to do by yourself. I decided to go back and try to reason you out of your fears."

"And when you got there I wasn't home."

"Right. And I stood around for a while, wondering if you had been foolish enough to have gone next door."

"Naturally, I'd been that dumb," I said, my voice heavy with an irony that David's guilty expression acknowledged.

"Yes, well . . ." and suddenly he was near me again, holding both my hands in his. "Oh, darling, if I hadn't gone — "

"I should have managed to have gotten the three of us out of the house anyway," I announced blithely, half-believing, half-skeptical.

But David believed me. "Yes, I think you would have done just that," he said, and then it didn't matter if it was true or not, as long as David might keep looking at me like that, holding me with his eyes in a way I never wanted to stop.

We were still, just gazing at each other for a while, and then David was clasping me to him as if I might vanish, and I was kissing him as if I never would.

"I think I might be getting involved," I whispered into his shirt front.

"You'd better be," he muttered, letting me go in deference to my aching head which seemed, just now, not to be troubling me at all.

"You," I began to admonish him, "how come there were all those long, long lapses when you never called me, and I had to — "

"Bring Peabody into my office as an excuse," he teased.

But I paid no attention to that. "Peabody," I squeaked, "is he — ?"

"He's here and quite happily too. Naturally, with Kate around. I even took his cast off for you — free of charge."

"Oh, David," I told him, lapsing back into sadness for a moment, "sometimes I really didn't think you cared for me at all."

He shook his head at me. "You have a lot to learn, Tanya."

That made me angry, but as I began to splutter at him, he shushed me with his words. "I was just afraid."

"Afraid?!"

"Yes," he said. "I'm thirty-seven, and you know very well how old you are. I was concerned that might be a big obstacle for us. Everything was happening so quickly for me, and I wanted to slow things down a bit."

"But you've changed your mind, huh?" I needled him, easily brushing aside any age problem. After all, there wasn't one.

"I didn't have any choice," he told me simply, and I hugged him to me, for a moment experiencing a real joy that there was a David Montserrat in the world and that he was very much mine.

And then I thought of Kate. Her parents were in jail — what had she been told? What was happening to her? What was she feeling and thinking?

"Kate," I said aloud. "What have you

told her? I've got to see her now, David."

"Whoa, one thing at a time," he cautioned me. "Kate's been helping me to look after you — in fact it took both of us to badger the doctor into letting you stay here and not go to the hospital. She'll be eager to see you too, Tanya, but there are a few things you should know first, and I think we've talked enough for a while."

I couldn't believe that David was serious, just willing to let me hang this way, everything in suspension, and expecting that I'd settle quietly down for a little nap.

"Just because you socked me into unconsciousness doesn't mean — " I began, and then felt awful as I saw him wince.

"I had to hit you, honey. You were getting in the way of letting me help you at all, you were so suspicious and frightened of me."

"I know," I told him, mollified and thinking how I'd really have to begin watching my prickly tongue. "But David, I couldn't rest now. Not yet, not till I know about Kate, what you told her."

"I told her the truth, Tanya. I had to. Oh, I was gentle, as much as I could be, at least. But she had to know. Actually, she took it quite well. I think she was relieved somehow. It was as if she'd known all along that something very wrong was going on, but didn't know what, or how to fix it."

I nodded. What David was saying confirmed feelings I'd had about Kate.

"She certainly had a mess of little 'foster' brothers and sisters to get used to taking care of," David said roughly, and I flinched, the enormity of what the Harrises had done flooding back to me.

"But Kate, how does she really — " I began, needing to know, no matter how bad it was.

"I'm not sure exactly what she's feeling, Tanya. She trusts me, but of course she doesn't know me all that well. When you talk to her you'll probably understand better than I do." He paused. "The thing is, and this of course Kate does know, the Harrises aren't her real parents."

"Oh, David, no! You don't mean that she — like the others — that she was . . ." I couldn't find the words. Kate! It would be too horrible to contemplate.

"No, no," David quickly quieted me. "They adopted her. All legal, nothing like what you're thinking," he said, and I breathed easier.

"I suppose they just needed a nursemaid," I said cruelly.

"Probably that was mostly it," David admitted, "but I think they — or at least Arlene — really grew fond of her." He ruffled my hair and kissed me on the cheek. "At least Kate's head seems to be in pretty good shape, which is more than we can say for you right now."

And at David's words, I realized quite suddenly how really exhausted I'd become. I must see Kate for myself, talk to her long and hard and lovingly. But just now, just now I didn't think I could manage it.

I felt David's hands sliding away from me. I was sinking back down against the pillows, and a lovely peace stole over me, letting me slip gently and comfortably into a calm, dreamless sleep.

CHAPTER NINETEEN

I was growing sleepy; we'd worked all day and had just finished trimming the tree, but Kate was overexcited, and I knew there was no way I was going to get her to go to bed easily, without a fight.

I yawned, pushing aside the curtains to watch a light snow drifting down over the lawn and frosting the pine trees so that the house looked, I knew, like a ginger-bread thing. The fire was not yet out, and because I knew I would have to stay awake till it was, I suggested to Kate that we have a cup of cocoa. Hopefully it would make her tired, and keep me awake. Although I don't know how I hoped a simple mug of hot chocolate would cure us both so easily and so differently.

"What time is David coming tomorrow?" Kate asked, fiddling with an errant pine cone on the tree with one hand and tossing Peabody a bit of tinsel to play with with the other.

"How many times does that make?" I said to her, and she gave me a hang-dog look that I couldn't resist.

"Oh, okay," I said, giving up, "he is coming, my dear Kate, at two o'clock, which is," I made a big pretense of rolling up my sleeve and looking at my watch, "only about fourteen hours away."

"I know," Kate said, knowing indeed. "I don't see how I'll be able to wait for that long."

"You could try sleeping part of it away," I suggested dryly.

"But, what about my chocolate?" Kate asked.

"Coming, coming, your ladyship," I said, skipping quickly from the living room into the kitchen and hearing Kate's giggles ringing behind me.

It was good to hear her laugh, since it had been scarcely two weeks ago when we'd been able to coax the first real smile from her. She'd been staying at the Rinns', with me, while David and I waited to see what the courts would do.

Then one night while I was trying to interest Kate in a particularly bad television show when David arrived, quite unexpected.

"I was afraid you two would be asleep," he said when I let him in, followed closely by Kate, who seemed to trail me everywhere those days. I thought that I must be the only real thing in her life to cling to; the one she hoped wouldn't escape her the way so many others had. I did my best to reassure her, and keep her calm while we were waiting.

"Not while we can watch a bad movie on TV, right?" I said, turning to include Kate.

She gave us both one of those crooked smiles she'd adopted lately, and which always made my heart beat irregularly. I was Kate once—oh, so many years ago. Needing to be wanted, to be cared for and loved. I knew that smile.

"Have you any champagne around, Tanya?" David asked, smiling happily at me to let me know all was well and very good. "We have something to celebrate, I think."

"Fresh out," I told him. "How about some flat cider and stale cookies?"

"Funny, isn't she?" David asked Kate, who was looking from one to the other of us, wondering what was up.

David put an arm around both of us and led us into the den, shutting off the TV with a mock shudder as he went.

"Sit down, you two," he ordered and we obeyed, Kate with her eyes fastened to David, whom I knew she regarded as something of a hero.

"I have plans to tell you, and I need you both to agree so that they'll work out." He looked over at Kate with a serious expression on has face. "You know that Tanya and I plan to be married, don't you, Kate?"

I gasped, not knowing how she could know, since I hadn't told her. But Kate was cannier than I had thought. She nodded solemnly at David.

"We're going to wait till the fall, till the Rinns come home to claim their house and Tanya's job here will be finished," he said, watching Kate who was also closely watching him.

"I've just been to Boston and talked to a judge there, for maybe the twentieth time." David grimaced at me, and then continued. "He said it will be fine for you to live here with Tanya and go to school as you've been doing. Is that all right with you, Kate?"

Kate told him that, yes, it was. And I looked, vainly, for some spark of happiness or pleasure in her tone. I could find none.

"Well," David went on, "then we come to this fall. What we'd like, Kate, what would make Tanya and me very happy, is if you'd think about continuing to live with us then." He wiped his forehead with his hand. The room was cool enough, no fire had been lighted, and I knew David was just having a problem saying this, making Kate believe what he really meant. "We'd like you to just keep on living with us till you're older and some man or career or both steals you." He stopped and then started again; I didn't risk looking at Kate. "We want to adopt you, Kate. If you'd like that . . . if you'll let us. I think the judge will want to talk to you about this too, but he's given me permission to tell you first." David finished, and I watched him fold back against his chair in relief.

And then I dared to look at Kate. At first there was that same lopsided smile on her face, and slowly, as I watched, it broke apart and her lips spread in a wide grin that lighted her eyes and warmed both David and me immeasurably.

It seemed we'd won, the three of us, and the next few minutes dissolved in a total confusion of hugging, kissing, and crying. All of us just holding on to each other and being happy.

I carried the chocolate, dotted with marshmallows, into the living room, hoping that Kate might have succumbed and I'd find her curled up asleep somewhere. But no. She was sitting on a low stool before the tree. She'd turned the tree lights on and was gazing up, enraptured — like a child on Christmas, I thought, setting the tray down quietly on the coffee table so I could watch her in silence. It was with a sudden jolt that I realized that that, of course, was just what she was.

I was making Kate a Christmas, possibly the nicest she'd ever known, and I was so terribly glad to be doing that. Tanya Sohier, nest-builder, was going to be a new role for me, but I decided I'd get plenty of enjoyment from it.

Kate swung around — the little stinker had known I was there all the time. She grinned at me mischievously. "Is David bringing you a ring tomorrow?" she asked, taking me back.

"What are you talking about?" I passed the cocoa, regarding her mildly, not willing to let her see that I was as excited as she was.

"Ohhhh, nothing," Kate replied nonchalantly, "except he ought to be coughing up something pretty soon, shouldn't he?"

"Kate!" I exclaimed, aghast, "is it Peabody who's teaching you those dreadful expressions?"

"Peabody!" She laughed at me. "He knows a lot worse than that, Tanya. His mouth is so foul that — "

"Never mind," I told her, having lived

through enough discourses between Kate and what used to be my cat. "I know all about his gutter talk. You needn't explain. In fact, sweetheart, all you need to do is finish your cocoa and get straight, right up to bed, or I swear I'll call David in the morning and tell him not to set foot in here till Christmas Day."

"You wouldn't!"

"I wouldn't?"

"Well, you probably wouldn't," Kate replied thoughtfully, "but I don't think I'm going to take any chances!" And she finished the rest of her cocoa in a gulp and jumped up, pausing to give me a smudgy kiss on the cheek before she and Peabody disappeared upstairs.

After she'd gone, I sat looking at the twinkling lights on the tree, feeling the snow falling deeply outside, and knowing a very real peace. I had a ready-made family, I thought drowsily, for the first time since my parents had died, I had a home and love around me — complete with a cat.

David, Kate, and I opened our packages on Christmas Eve night after a huge dinner of goose and trimmings that had turned out perfectly.

Kate was rosy and fairly bouncing with pleasure over the gifts that the two of us had carefully selected for her — mostly clothes which she so badly needed and wanted, and a large leather handbag I'd seen her eyeing covetously in town, with a soft kid wallet to go with it, into which David had slyly inserted a spanking new ten-dollar bill. Kate was ecstatic.

At the last minute I'd given into myself and bought her a great hulking orange, pink, and brown turtle I'd seen in the window of a toy store in Boston, hoping that she was still young enough to think it was great. Secretly, I thought it was pretty terrific myself. And so did Kate.

"Tanya!" she exclaimed, tearing off the tissue paper, "it's perfect! It's just what I've always wanted." And David and I smiled at each other happily, thankful that after everything Kate was still young and untouched enough to feel this way.

"Now David," she addressed him quite seriously, "you give Tanya yours. Your real present. Come on."

"You mean . . ." David pretended surprise, "I have to give *her* something too? This whole holiday wasn't thought up especially for you?"

"Very funny," Kate rebuked him, and I felt my heart rapping around again, only this time it was with happy excitement.

David fumbled in his pockets, to Kate's delight, pretending he had forgotten something, or lost it. And then at last he came up with a tiny package, wrapped in silvery paper with a tiny sprig of mistletoe stuck into its gold-ribboned bow.

"Merry Christmas, darling," he said, coming over to sit next to me as I shakily undid the wrappings.

"Tanya, I bet I can guess — "

"Shut up!" I warned Kate, glaring at her as fiercely as I could. A look that had little effect on her — except for this time. She just sat back sedately, if knowingly, and watched me unwrap David's engagement ring.

I opened the lid of the box carefully and looked down through a blur of tears at the ring David had chosen.

"Oh, David," I breathed, leaning against him and holding onto his hand, "it's perfect. It's so perfect, it's perfectly beautiful!"

David hugged me to him and then glanced over at Kate. "So what do you think, Kate? Do you think she thinks it's perfect or not?"

I swatted out at him as Kate said, "But, Tanya, you haven't even *looked* at it yet!"

Of course she was right and I hadn't, really. I blinked my eyes and focused them down at the ring, rising from the white velvet of the box. I'd been right anyhow, it was beautiful — a thin gold band which coiled around to be the setting for an oval-shaped emerald which glittered back at me, reflecting the myriad lights of the Christmas tree.

David slipped it out of the box and onto my finger, kissing me on the ear, and whispering, "I love you."

"Well," Kate got up, yawning so fakely at us that I had to struggle not to laugh. "Hercules and I have got to get to bed if we expect to be up in time to visit David's parents tomorrow."

"Hercules?" I questioned her, and then saw that she was holding the turtle I'd given her and snuggling her head into it.

"Good night, Kate honey," I said, getting up to go over and hold her close, David joining me to drop a kiss on Kate's forehead. "I'm glad we belong to each other."

"Me too," she smiled happily at us.

After Kate had gone upstairs, David gathered me to him. "You're nice, my Tanya," he told me, holding me loosely in his arms. "Very nice."

And of course I knew I really would be just that from then on. All my spikes and thorns were already turning to gentle leaves. It was an amazing thing I had accomplished, I thought, taming all the parts of me I hated, giving and taking love. For the first time since I was fifteen I'd given love — to David, to Kate, and had been met head on with their warmth and caring. I felt a new softness begin to make my leaves grow.

On Christmas morning, before David was to pick us up, I began a letter to Anne. One I'd put off writing this long — until I was absolutely sure. And now I was.

"Dear Anne and Raymond,
"You're never going to believe what's *really* been happening to me these last few months. . . ."